W9-ABE-319

Isabelle

Marcelle LAGESSE

Marcelle Lagesse is a distinguished historian and a prolific novelist and playwright. She has received numerous literary awards. *Isabelle* was originally published in Mauritius in 1959 and was nominated the best novel of the Indian Ocean Isles by the French PEN Club. She lives in Phoenix, Mauritius.

Isabelle

Marcelle LAGESSE

Translated by James Kirkup
With a Preface by Anthony Blond

Quartet Books

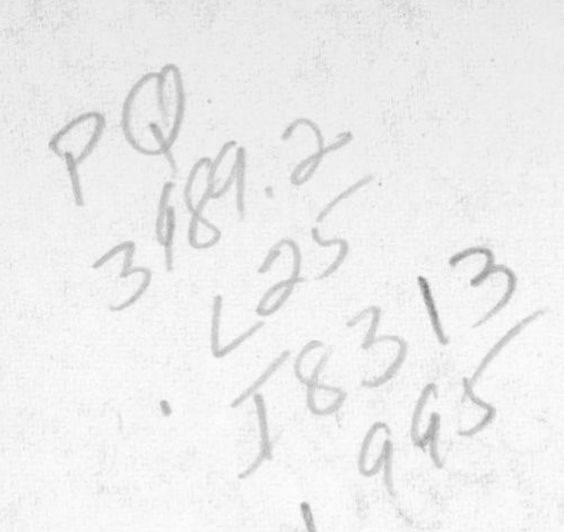

First published in Great Britain by Quartet Books Limited 1995
A member of the Namara Group
27 Goodge Street, London W1P 2LD

A catalogue record for this title is available from the British Library

ISBN 0 7043 0240 3

Printed and bound in Finland by WSOY

Preface

First published in Mauritius in 1959, when Frances Partridge gave it to me, it was its provenance that struck me: Editions Smith, in the remotest English possession where the descendants of French settlers and their imported artisans spoke the language of the *ancien régime* and lived tranquilly under a British administration. The book won two prizes, was reprinted twice in Paris and was later republished in Mauritius.

My recollection, of nearly forty years ago, was that the story turned on the love of the French daughter of a plantation owner for an English officer which had not been allowed, so they eloped at dawn in a stagecoach. I was quite wrong – it is much more subtle – but then Graham Greene forgot his own plots.

A planter, François Kerubec III, is found shot dead in the prime of life in the woods outside his handsome house, which is full of fine furniture and treasures. On the island, the murder is attributed to a light-skinned black slave avenging himself on the system, though François Kerubec had been the kindest of masters.

Nicolas Kerubec, François' cousin and a small-time lawyer from Nantes, arrives in 1833 to take up his inheritance. His estate, which produces cloves and cane sugar, is in good order thanks to the stewardship of an old family servant – a slave called Rantanplan. (The British Government, under pressure from the West Indies lobby in Westminster, is trying to abolish slavery in Mauritius – an island in commercial competition with the West Indies. Nicolas falls for his neighbour, a widow called Isabelle Ghast, who still has her youth and beauty and whose husband – a bullying drunk – died of a heart-attack (or was it something else?) ten years previously.

The settlers live an elegant and social life, the women happily consorting with British officers whom they occasionally marry. Nicolas is planning to buy Isabelle's neighbouring estate. Their intimacy is being noticed. An old family friend, Mme Boucard (she travels around in a palanquin and hates the English), urges Nicolas to sort out François' papers. When questioned by Nicolas about Isabelle, Madame Boucard, after some hesitation, replies: 'God forgive me, I do not like that woman. I have never liked that woman.' Nicolas remains tantalized by Isabelle, by her alternate cruelty and tenderness, openness yet evasiveness, and her constant beauty and courage. (She bathes alone in the sea at night.)

One night after a storm, Nicolas returns to his house to find Isabelle has taken refuge in one of the bedrooms. His passion is fulfilled. She leaves before dawn disguised as a man, having discarded her own clothes. A few days later, Nicolas hears that she has ordered that a slave be given thirty lashes. He then finds an unfinished letter from his cousin François describing his obsession for, and fear of, an unknown lady . . . He chances upon a strangely familiar dress among François' clothes . . . Isabelle's pistol is found by a slave in a marsh which Nicolas is draining . . . Nicolas arranges a meeting with Isabelle to confront her . . . She boards the stagecoach which leaves at dawn . . .

Anthony Blond

I

I used to feel as though everything happened according to routine on those evenings. But today, I'm not so sure.

I'm trying to recapture my father's voice, his intonations, his gestures as he opened the envelope. No matter when the letter arrived, we had to wait until the lime-blossom tisane was served after dinner in the library. I'm trying to recreate the atmosphere of those evenings. I'm going over in my mind, time and again, how things were in a period of my life that has been superseded forever. The life of an only son that flowed on so calmly. A life as easy as the course of waters running towards the sea.

I'm not so sure. I'm trying to rediscover other intonations of my father's voice, making comparisons. I can see my mother also. That slightly hunched posture, as if in apprehension. And the glow of the lamplight on their faces.

I'm listening to a letter being read in a low voice. Sometimes my father repeats a phrase more slowly. Today I realize it was to give weight not to the words but to the dreams with which he loaded those words. Or perhaps I'm reading too much into it now. You can never be sure. You grope your way through life and when you turn back, you find it's too late.

Our demesne slopes right down to the sea. From the terrace I can see the long avenue of palms and mirobolanos leading down to the shore. The ancient beams of the attic floors make cracking sounds under the hot sun. And there are those dresses in camphor in a chest, up there.

On evenings when the sheets of paper from that island were spread out on the little table between us, when the summer dusk softly shadowed the corners of the room – or when the logs were crackling in the hearth in winter – I would often wonder what life in the colonies must be like.

Twenty-nine . . . That figure is not given in self-defence. At twenty-nine, you know exactly what you want and what you cannot accept. I raise my eyes: the sea stretching to infinity . . . I know it was a choice I was allowed to make. A return to France, the life of a provincial notary, like that of my father, and of my grandfather before him: respectable and comfortable.

They told me that the roadstead I crossed, leaning on the deck rails, head bent over that less tempestuous deep, was once protected, in the early years of colonization, by the crossfire of gun emplacements and by a heavy chain that was stretched between the two forts at night. A century had gone by and I entered the port without trouble. I simply had to cross the bar during the night. And my whole life might have taken a different direction if some official had not done his job properly, if a postbag had fallen into the sea, if a ship had been wrecked. I should not have broken the red wax of these seals – and I should not have come here.

At Saint-Nazaire I should have carried on the family name, the family business. For which I had been brought up. In the old stone house, blackened and weatherbeaten, austere, with narrow windows, I should be seated still beside the hearth. Each morning, I should have sat down behind the desk that belonged to my grandfather. Guillaume, who had also been my father's head clerk, would have laid out dossiers before me; the Z estate, the Y estate, auction sales. I should have spent my afternoons at the club and in the evenings . . .

Yes, indeed, I could have been another man. But I crossed that threshold, I leaned on the wrought iron balustrade of the balcony, I stood at the foot of the great canopied bed.

Just as, probably, in days gone by and for more obvious reasons, the elder brother of my grandfather, François Kerubec, sub-lieutenant on a merchantman of the East India Company, was captured and detained here.

A print I found on the drawing-room wall recalls that a century ago the first colonizers camped in tents at Port Louis. There was a great deal of activity around the roadstead where vessels were anchored. Wearing the tricorne, naval or army officers stood arguing facing the port; others unrolled maps. Woodcutters were clearing the undergrowth. At the entrance to one of the tents, a woman was seated, holding her child by the hand. And that his how I like to imagine Catherine Couessin, wife of François Kerubec, the first of that name.

'Men are born Asiatics, Europeans, French, English,' wrote Bernardin de Saint-Pierre.* 'They are farmers, merchants, soldiers; but in whatever country they are born, women live and die as women.' I shall not express any opinion on that. I'm trying to bring back to life the woman who was the very heart and soul of this house before she was laid to rest beneath a grassy grave surmounted by a simple cross of hewn stone, across the stream there, in the land that belonged to her. I can almost see her dress moving among the clove trees, but upon the face I have invented for her I impose another face. And her presence in this abode . . . But that will suffice for the moment. I have neither the wish nor the courage to go on at present.

From the letters written by François, the third in the family line, there breathes a profound happiness, at once a sense of exaltation in his love of nature, and also, at times, an even deeper note. I remember certain phrases that struck me by their unexpected turns, which did not appear to bother my parents – but can I be so sure of that after all?

This for example: 'The day and the evening have been exquisite. Do you know anything more beautiful, more uplifting than drops of water running down bare skin?'

But we learned little enough about the man himself. Today I am no wiser. People have told me certain things, others have let me put two and two together. My imagination has done the rest. After the death of his father, he wrote to us regularly for several years, then came a period when our letters remained without reply, until the time arrived when we, too, stopped writing.

I've not been able to find those letters. Perhaps my father destroyed them after reading them; or perhaps my mother did so, fearing some sort of spell cast by the islands.

When my parents had passed away, I remember having searched for

* Famous French writer (1737–1814), author of the schoolroom classic *Paul et Virginie* (1788), an exotic childhood idyll set on Mauritius

those letters as if I already knew that one day, seated at the very table where they had been written, I should be racking my brains as I delved into that past of his. If I still possessed them, perhaps I should have been able to find the true meaning of that other phrase that nags at me continuously and that I try in vain to fathom. Sometimes, I seem to sense it floating around me, I can feel it concealed in the folds of the heavy silken curtains or running along the terrace with all its secrets explained: '. . . if I did not tremble at your self-assurance, if I did not have to tell myself that I must never dare question you . . .'

II

I took possession of the residence: 'A substantial dwelling, single-storeyed, built in the style of former days when one made it a labour of love, as did your ancestor, to assure the prosperity of his demesne,' as our family notary Leperet had written. 'He had obtained the concession of the land in 1735. An estate of one hundred hectares to begin with, situated on the outskirts of Mahébourg, which was then called Port Bourbon, in the district of Grand Port. Since 1735, the direct descendants of François Kerubec have made aquisitions of certain neighbouring terrains and today your estate is one of the largest on the island. It comprises sugar-cane and clove plantations – hence the property's name – coffee plantations and fields of pineapples which in that region grow without any need to tend them. The climate is agreeable. Your black dependants, about one hundred in number, are devoted servants. As I informed you at the beginning of this letter, it was against a light-skinned black, one of the last rivals of Ratsitatane probably, that the authorities have made the accusation of murder by firearms. My deeply mourned client . . .'

Trying to look back into the past, to weigh up the facts from the start of the affair, I find myself confronted by difficulties at every turn, I keep trying to bring to light things that perhaps are of no importance, I get confused. I am tempted to put it all behind me, unwilling to persevere in my task, in all that forces me back into my enslavement to the mystery.

But that January morning in 1833, in Nantes, I was roaming through the snowy streets feeling like someone who, without any effort on his part, is seeing the realization of what had been only an impossible dream. My luggage had been loaded on board the *Minerva*, captained by Habelin, which was to set sail in the afternoon. I was embarking for Mauritius without the slightest qualm, without any sense of anxiety. The demesne, my inheritance, was flourishing. My practice in Saint-Nazaire had been left in the care of Jean Desprairie for two years. It had been agreed that he would take it over if I had not returned before the end of that period. I ran through the streets of Nantes like a schoolboy starting a holiday.

Naturally, I felt sad, thinking of the tragic end of my cousin François, found one morning with a bullet through his heart in a remote corner of his estate. I was indignant that those whose duty it was to arrest the murderer had not yet done so. I believed that if I were there, on the spot, I should have been implacable in my judgement. I loved François as one loves everything that makes a deep impression on one or seems to be in a sphere above one's own: it was with a mixture of tenderness and awe, of admiration and reticence. He was fifteen years older than I; he was my childhood hero.

That January morning I kept thinking that François was dead, that I was inheriting his land, his slaves, his house, his fortune – that from being a modest provincial notary I had become a landed proprietor. I was embarking upon a good, solid ship of the line; I had reserved one of her best cabins and felt as though I held the whole world in my hands.

We raised anchor on a sunless afternoon, without my having been able to make out who were my travelling companions among all those who crowded the deck, giving farewell embraces, offering advice which I caught in passing without knowing who had offered it nor to whom it was addressed. I went down to my cabin, opened my bags and prepared myself for a voyage that would last three or four months. Through the porthole I could still see the quayside of France. A woman, with a graceful movement, lifted her dress slightly to step over some obstacle. She raised her hand and waved at someone up on the bridge. Just then the anchor chain began rolling round the capstan, a bell was ringing. I could hear the ropes squealing in the pulleys, then suddenly the slow waltzing of the ship began. Orders were given through a megaphone and repeated by a member of the crew. I was thinking I should have to go and present myself to the captain before dinner.

The voyage passed without incident. Week after monotonous week.

Sometimes we were becalmed for two or three days in the same latitude. The sails drooped from the masts and the sailors cast their fishing lines. The vessel rolled. To conquer my boredom I played *écarté* for hours on end.

Among the passengers was a former paymaster of the Ile de France* who had taken up residence on the Ile Bourbon after the Ile de France had been captured by the English, and who was returning to his plantations. He was accompanied by his wife and by his cousins (two young newlyweds who had been tempted by colonial life), by a new estate manager and his wife, by a twenty-year-old nephew and a servant. One was always bumping into one or other of them and the other passengers often got the impression that Monsieur Bourtin and his entourage had chartered the vessel for their personal use. On the very first evening out I had struck up a friendship with another passenger, a former naval captain, Souville, a pleasant seventy-year-old gentleman. Resident on Mauritius for about thirty years, he liked to talk about his campaigns, above all those in which he had served under the orders of rear-admiral Sercey. He would also recall the flagships captured by Surcouf and was still indignant that the *Emile* had been denied a *lettre de marque*.

'To think that he was only twenty and not a pirate like the rest of them. A hundred and eighty tons, only a hundred and eighty tons, four canon, thirty men and six captures right away.'

He had been present at the seizure of the island by the English. Unlike Monsieur Bourtin he had not enjoyed the benefits of article IX of the treaty of surrender that allowed the settlers on the Ile de France 'to be granted a period of two years in which to leave the colony with their possessions'.

But in Souville's presence you could not mention the battle of Grand Port in which he had not been able to take part, having been confined to his bed – 'yes, just knocked up by a high fever'. In 1810 he hesitated somewhat, but in the end stayed on in Mauritius.

Day after endless day, sitting in armchairs on the deck of the *Minerva*, staring at the ocean, we would spend hours in idle talk. It was from him that I acquired the initial information about political, economic and social life on the island. Most of the colonials who had landed there during the previous century, like my cousins, had put down roots.

* Original name of Mauritius

Property passed from father to son. The colonizers' descendants led lives of a certain grandeur and visitors would tell tales of their generous hospitality. Souville would trot out such details and a thousand more in an inconsequential manner under the equatorial sun, or at night beneath swarms of stars. The days and nights slipped by slowly and I had to keep my impatience in check. The passage of the line injected a little gaiety among those on board who were crossing the equator for the first time and received their baptismal certificates duly signed by Neptune. That old seadog Souville presided over the event.

As time went by a similar cast of thought bound the old man and myself ever closer together day after day. It was he who, later, despite his great age, hastened to answer my appeal for help and granted me the boon of his presence without any name having to be mentioned.

But in any case, who could have done more for me than I myself? For long months, week had followed week. In July, there was the sugar-cane to be cut and to be despatched to the refinery at Beau Vallon. Rising at dawn, going to bed well after nightfall, after having seen to everything throughout the long day, ready for the morrow, I would sleep like a brute beast. I've more leisure now. Sometimes, seated on the terrace, with my pipe as constant companion, I watch the fine carriages passing by and, judging by the direction they take, I can tell whether they are making for Beau Vallon, Ferney or Riche-en-Eau. I can imagine their elegantly dressed, scented ladies, hair in a smooth chignon, shoulders bare, bejewelled. I invent their conversations, I dream of their coquettish ways, their calculating smiles. Such images haunt my thoughts.

On the road, the carriage moves away behind its trotting horses, a light still flashing from it, then disappears. I think that another man would perhaps have taken that road one night with his companion. On returning home he would have fallen asleep, his heart filled with the happiness of possessing a ravishing and devoted woman, and would not have woken up.

François too must have sat here in the same place on the terrace. He, like me, would have heard the carriages and watched them passing in the distance. Perhaps – who can tell? – it was on such a night that he wrote the letter or that draft of a letter which I keep under lock and key, in a secret drawer in his writing-desk? Once again, I'm full of conflicting thoughts, once again I'm mulling over my ceaseless torment.

I believe I acted out to the full the role of a seeker after justice but at a price that concerns me alone.

Yes, it was an uneventful voyage. At the Cape of Good Hope, we took on board Lavoye, the surgeon. Two weeks later we reached the Ile Bourbon. The Bourtins and their entourage left me with a thousand protestations of eternal friendship, and I even believe, God forgive me, that I invited them to come and visit me on Mauritius.

On Sunday 21 April, at the first shout of 'land ahoy' from the watch, I was up on the bridge and unable to control my excitement. But two long hours had to pass before we were able to make out anything more than a brownish line on the horizon. Nevertheless, I was filled with joy and pride. On the poop, following the directions of Captain Habelin, I had seized a telescope and was trying to distinguish the mountains: Piton de la Rivière Noire, Morne Brabant, Mont Rempart . . . A white line encircled the coast.

'What about the Mont du Lion, d'you see the Mont du Lion?' Souville asked me slyly. He knew that my estate lay at the foot of that mountain. But the Mont du Lion was much further to the east and we had arrived right on the Rivière Noire. I had to resign myself to not being able to salute my possessions as we sailed by. Towards four, the wind veered and a fresh tack made us retreat prudently out to sea again. We tried to hide our mutual disappointment.

Despite everything that took place subsequently, I retain a clear memory of our last night on board. We had shortened sail and the entire crew had assembled on deck after dinner. We hardly exchanged a word. On the forecastle, stretched out on a sheet of canvas stiffened by seawater, four or five sailors were singing old Breton folk songs. The words with their harsh syallables took possession of the night, they seemed to run across the surface of the ocean, hit the crests of the waves and leap in bursts of spray. The ship rolled from starboard to larboard. We had the impression of living through an endless panse, as if, having almost arrived at the end of our voyage, something that for nearly three months had held us together as one was about to dissolve and deliver us up to the tempest.

That night, I stayed on deck a long time. The Southern Cross that I had learned to identify was sparkling in the heavens. All the ship's sounds died away one by one and soon there was nothing to be heard but the footsteps of the officer on watch on the bridge – our guardian angel.

III

I awoke late. When I left my cabin, the ship was entering the port to drop anchor among fifty or so other vessels. In the town, still fortified and built at the foot of the chain of mountains encircling it, traders and ships' chandlers were thronging the streets, making contacts with others from every corner of the globe. I learned later that the town was as big as Nantes, but the first thing that struck me when I disembarked, even though I had already been advised of the fact, was the mixture of races on the quayside. The entire Orient was represented and the diversity of costumes amazed me. I was even more astonished as I realized that everyone seemed to know everyone else, that they were all talking to one another and – miraculously – understood one another. Souville was amused by my reactions.

A dozen coachmen rushed towards us. The problem of choosing was spared us, for the most enterprising of them, sporting an improbable top hat, had seized our luggage. I have since become familiar with the Mauritian *patois* derived from French and can now speak it fluently. I know that *vous* is *ou*, that *toi* is *to*, that the verb to love is expressed by *content*, perhaps to indicate felicity. But that first morning that resonant form of speech and its sing-song intontations surprised me agreeably. Everything, indeed, was surprise. I found that I should have to spend two days at the Hôtel Masse, as the stagecoach for the Grand Port left only on Wednesdays and Saturdays.

Nothing has changed. In the evenings, the trot of horses reverberates on the road and something like a responsive echo or a sob trembles here in the house when they pass by. I feel as if I know now that the house itself, like its owner, is remembering. That it is divided, as I am, between remorse and salvation, and that it is forgiving me for being a weaker vessel brooding on its pain, taking pleasure in it, and making of it the essence of his days.

As soon as we had arrived at the hotel, Souville wrote to his children to let them know of his safe arrival and of his intention to remain with me in Port Louis until the Wednesday. In turn, I apprised my lawyer, Leperet, of my arrival and begged him to come and see me the next day. The hotel management was charged with the delivery of the letters, and Souville's was sent post-haste by pony express to Pamplemousses.

On the first floor, our rooms opened directly on to a balcony where there flowered a collection of geraniums – the hotel proprietor's pride and joy. Facing us, we had the rich foliage of the East India Company Gardens. Lunch was brought up to our rooms and Souville and I agreed to visit certain parts of the town that afternoon.

We had no definite itinerary. 'We shall walk down the rue de Castries, our street,' Souville told me, 'towards the *levée*, known as the Chaussée. You'll see Government House better than we did this morning from the ship, and then we can perhaps proceed as far as the Champ de Mars.'

It was very hot, and despite my lack of sleep during the night, I slept badly during my siesta. I finally got up around four o'clock and donned a light summer walking suit. All was quiet in the hotel. As I was going towards Souville's room I passed a young woman in the corridor; she was the first woman I had encountered in Mauritius. I noted that she was of slight build and fairly lively in her movements, which made me smile because I was thinking of the notorious indolence of the Creoles of whom our host, Monsieur Masse, was a shining example. Since our arrival that morning, he had not budged from his veranda. Stretched out in a chaise-longue, he appeared nevertheless to have an eye to everything, for, from time to time, imperious blasts on a whistle would bring slaves running to his side to receive and execute his commands.

I had been amazed to find such a luxurious and well-kept hotel at Port Louis. We Europeans have our own mistaken ideas about the colonies. We see them only through the eyes of Bernardin de

Saint-Pierre, who described to us houses roofed with straw on the slopes of the mountain, broad-leaved banana trees, loyal black servants . . .

As we were crossing the veranda, Monsieur Masse called out to us: 'It is with the greatest pleasure that I welcome the cousin of Monsieur François Kerubec. Your cousin was one of my best clients. He often stayed at Port Louis during the racing season, for he had a passion for horses, as you know.'

I did not venture to acquaint him with the fact that I did not know a great deal about my cousin's life and that our host was the first person to have spoken to me about François in such detail. I made some vague response but he did not listen and rattled on.

'I've just been talking about your cousin to Madame Isabelle Ghast whom I have had the honour of counting among my guests for the last few days. She is one of your neighbours – of course there can be no comparison between your estate and hers! But I hope you will not be thinking me indiscreet. This is an island one could almost hold in the palm of one's hand and naturally everyone knows everything that is going on. You had no sooner disembarked this morning than we were told that the sole remaining relative of François Kerubec had arrived to take possession of his inheritance. Is it not so, captain, that nothing can be kept secret here?' he added, turning towards Souville.

I answered Monsieur Masse that there was no reason for me to go incognito and I also assured him that I fully intended to work my own land and possibly to introduce new methods of cultivation.

'That's the sort of man I like,' replied Monsieur Masse, 'determined to press ahead, whatever the cost, with courage and fortitude. Just think – there was a rumour going round this morning that you were going to sell your estate. You have my very best wishes, Monsieur, my very best wishes. Are you intending to visit the town? May I ask you two gentlemen to be so good as to sign the register on your return? We did not want to bother you with it this morning, after your three months at sea.'

His plump, dimpled hand was leisurely plying a fan. We took leave of him, promising that we should not hesitate to address ourselves to him should we require anything special or if we had complaints to make about his slaves.

It was while we were wandering down the streets of Port Louis that afternoon that Souville spoke to me about Mahé de la Bourdonnais and about the genius this governor had displayed during his governorship of the Ile de France.

'Though he did not succeed in bringing everything to a fruitful conclusion,' said Souville as we passed through the gates to the hotel, 'he laid the foundations for many of the subsequent developments, and prepared numerous plans. Take this *levée* and the East India Company Gardens, would you believe that in 1735 the sea covered them at high tide, stirring up all the mud lying stagnant? La Bourdonnais undertook to fill in this part of Port Louis not just to sanitize the town but also to create what you see before you now. The works were not completed in his time. Though the Company's garden dates from the first years of colonization, the rest of the marshland was for a long time impracticable. It is said that the inhabitants from different districts in the town cast large stones into the marsh thus building a sort of causeway that reduced the distance to be covered between the eastern and the western suburbs. By extending the work begun by La Bourdonnais, this is what has been accomplished.'

Today the Chaussée is the principle commercial artery of the port. The finest shops are found along it. At one end stands the main gate of the Barracks, at the other we find Government House, on the Place d'Armes which stretches down to the ocean.

'The main buildings constructed under La Bourdonnais are Government House, the Barracks, the Palais de Justice, the hospital and the forts and warehouses – all handed over intact to the English at the surrender,' Souville added.

We walked down to the port. The *Minerva*, at anchor, was surrounded by lighters. We knew that as soon as her cargo had been unloaded the vessel was to be laid up in the graving dock of *Trou Fanfaron* for refitting. Souville informed me that, once again, it was La Bourdonnais who had the idea of providing for the construction and repair of ships on the Ile de France. As he had at his disposal only a few qualified craftsmen, he started a system of apprenticing to his French workmen a certain number of blacks. The result was so satisfactory that after a while the high reputation of the Ile de France for the construction of highly rated long-distance vessels equalled that of Lorient. In less than five years, keeping the promise he had made to the East India Company, La Bourdonnais had created an ideal port of call in the Indian Ocean. From the quayside we could contemplate all the activity of the port. Lighters were provisioning vessels with water and firewood.

'It's sad to think that man died miserably, that he was rewarded only by ingratitude, hatred and incomprehension,' said Souville. 'He spent twenty-eight months in solitary confinement in the Bastille. When he was finally rehabilitated, his health was broken and he was ruined. He died two years later, leaving his family destitute. Subsequently, the Colonial Assembly of the Ile de France paid an annual pension of three thousand pounds to the daughter of Mahé de la Bourdonnais. The settlers on the Ile de France considered tht they were simply paying a sacred debt of gratitude by making thus a public acknowledgement of veneration for the founder of the colony. It should not be forgotten that after they took the island the English insisted on reinstating that pension which had been cancelled when the Colonial Assembly was abolished in 1803. These are details which perhaps do not interest you, but I am a living witness of such things. Forgive your old friend for having talked about them at such length.'

I assured him that far from being tedious, his information would help me to adapt more quickly.

'One does not adopt a country,' I said, 'and one is not adopted by one if one does not know its past, its hours of glory or decline and its weaknesses. Naturally, as we had relatives on the Ile de France we were concerned by everything related to this colony, but at such a great distance one is not well informed. As I look upon these sites today, telling myself that those who preceded us suffered, laboured and died to open the way for us, and for all those who are to come here, I become conscious of a strange feeling. All these things that remain, that endure, make me feel like a mortal who does not want to die. In Europe, in our cities and in our smallest villages even, we do not enjoy this sense of creation. It would seem that if there is no beginning there is no sequel. But here, ever since this morning, at every step I take I encounter something that once began, that still has its history and at times also its mystery.'

Souville gazed upon the port. 'Would you believe it,' he asked me, 'if I say that since I first dropped anchor here thirty-seven years ago, I have never regretted taking up residence here. A voyage to France every two or three years – perhaps this time it's the final return – that is enough for me. I'd roughed it around the globe so much that I finally longed for a bit of peace and quiet. Where else but here could I have found such happiness? Come, let's take a stroll down the rue de l'Intendance.'

I was glad to find, despite twenty-three years of English occupation, a French atmosphere on Mauritius. The speech, the names of streets, the interest I read in the glances of those we met, the exclamations when people recognized Souville and stopped to talk to him, asking him for the latest news from France, and what he thought of the new monarchy under the government of Thiers, all led me to the realization that everyone here lived with their eyes turned towards their former homeland – even the Creoles who had never left the island.

In front of the cathedral we met the funeral procession of a black slave. A few friends were accompanying the coffin of white wood that was placed upon two rounded stones on the square in front of the church. A priest in a surplice was hurrying towards them.

After our stroll, we ended up at the Champ de Mars as night was falling. In the twilight the site was one of unbelievable majesty. The mountain chain encircling the plain still makes me think today of an immense Coliseum hewn by giants out of sheer rock. We walked back to the hotel slowly; the evening air was pleasant.

It was not without sadness that I contemplated our coming separation. My companion used to say that I reminded him, though some years older, of his grandson whom he had accompanied back to France.

IV

As soon as we got back to the hotel, we made haste to sign the register as we had been asked. It lay upon a little table in the entrance hall. Souville signed his name and went up to his room. I amused myself reading the last two or three pages before taking up the pen. I came upon the name of Isabelle Ghast, née Comiane, landed properietor at Grand Port, arrived 7 April at the hotel. So she had been in Port Louis for two weeks. It struck me that she had known François, that they were perhaps friends and must have seen one another often. I carefully inscribed my name, with a certain naïve pride: Nicolas Kerubec, landed proprietor at Grand Port, arrived in Mauritius 22 April 1833, aboard the *Minerva*.

When I raised my eyes, the young woman I had encountered in the corridor was on the landing of the first floor and just at that moment began to come down the stairs. We passed one another on the first step of the staircase. On the landing I automatically turned to look back: she was bent over the register.

Meals were served on small individual tables in a vast dining room whose french windows gave on to the garden. A dozen or so people, including two ladies, were already dining when Souville and I installed ourselves at the table that had been reserved for us. A couple – who left the colony the next day – occupied the table on our right. The other lady, she of the corridor, who I had learnt was my neighbour at Grand Port, was eating alone opposite me, sitting bolt upright on her chair, her eyes gazing at the tropic night through the open doors. She appeared so utterly absorbed by her thoughts that I was able to study her at leisure. I did not find her beautiful in the strict sense of the term but she was of exquisite distinction. She had brown eyes slanting a little towards the temples and this particularity appeared to make the lower part of her face look thinner. The nose was straight, the mouth generous, but with well-modelled lips. Her dark chestnut hair was pulled back in a heavy chignon on the nape of her neck, but a few stray curls peeping from the bandeau round her brow and temples caught the light and cast a sort of halo around her face. She was wearing a dress of grey material with a high collar fastened by a jewelled clasp. A sober costume, almost of monastic severity, softened by a froth of lace round the cuffs, making each of her gestures like the flight of a seagull.

'You're very far away, dear boy,' Souville suddenly remarked.

'I was wondering if the face is the mirror of the soul.'

'Well, you know, there have been assassins with angel faces and brutish features on men who were gentle as lambs. On the *Venus* that was under my command when I arrived here on 21 June 1796 . . .'

But Madame Ghast was rising from her table. We bowed to her as she passed close by us.

'Very agreeable neighbourhood,' grunted Souville.

My eyes followed the long pale grey robe.

'Now if you had seen the face of the quarter-master on that ship, my boy . . .'

I was never to hear the story of the quarter-master, for that was the moment when our host swept into the room, a letter in his hand, and spoke to Souville: 'Why did you not warn me this morning, captain, because you knew about it, didn't you? You could not have been ignorant of the fact, arriving from Europe? You could not have been unaware that he had embarked! What's to become of us? Ruined, all our possessions will be dispersed. After having worked all our lives!'

He then decided to read us the letter. It had arrived by the *Minerva* and he had left it lying on the table all day. In it he was given warning from the Ile Bourbon that a correspondent in England had announced the return of John Jérémie to Mauritius and specified that he had embarked upon the *Jupiter*, a ship of the line.

I gathered that John Jérémie had already spent some time on the island colony in 1832. He had arrived with the title and authority of

Attorney General and was empowered to apply the law voted in November 1831, a law proclaiming the emancipation of the slaves, without indemnity.

'So as to get rid of him – you remember, captain – we all refused to do any work for forty days. Yes, sir, everything was closed down. The butchers stopped going to the abattoirs, the vegetables shrivelled in the gardens, the ships in the harbour could neither load nor discharge cargo. We had a hard time of it, but thank the Lord we emerged victorious from that confrontation. And now we'll have to start all over again! Coming here and accusing us of treating our slaves in the most inhuman manner! They'd already set over us their Slave Protector and we had submitted to him. I can't help thinking there's something else behind all this.'

'My dear Masse,' said one of the diners, 'what's behind it all is that the West Indies can no longer tolerate the presence of Mauritian sugar on the European markets. What they want is to cut at the very root of the problem, and bring about the ruin of the Mauritian traders. As you know, the West Indies have a number of friends in the anti-slavery campaign. Ah! talk about human philanthropy!'

'Monsieur Kerubec,' went on Monsieur Masse, 'you have just disembarked, you will be seeing things with fresh eyes. Well then, I must take you to Camp Libre and you'll see a great number of blacks whom their masters emancipated out of goodness of heart. Can you imagine such a thing? As for me, if they took away my slaves without paying me compensation, I should be reduced to begging in the streets.'

It was amusing to hear the proprietor of such a fine three-storey hotel talking to us of his approaching ruin as he paced the marble-flagged floors of his dining room. The diners had drawn their chairs together and soon everyone was talking. The hotelier's vehemence made us chuckle, but I could tell by the attitude of the others that the situation could not but appear very serious.

'So he must have left London before the arrival of d'Epinay,' someone said.

Then they began to give dates and count the number of days. Other people arrived shortly and the discussion turned upon the measures to be taken to prevent the disembarkation of the man whom all the colonists regarded as their enemy.

'Let us not forget the famous pamphlet he published in 1831,' said a gentleman with side-whiskers, 'and the famous phrase of Robespierre he dinned into our ears: "Let the colonies perish, rather than let a principle die!"'

A few days after I had moved into Girofliers, I heard that John Jérémie had disembarked at Port Louis on 29 April with – as an added precaution – five hundred troops. The next day, he took up his post of Attorney General and began his career on Mauritius by insulting a bailiff and displaying disrespect to the Court.

That evening, when the imminent return of John Jérémie had become known, consternation could be seen on every face, could be sensed in every conversation. A new Governor, Sir William Nicolay, had arrived two months ago in the colony and his first repressive measure against those who had led the campaign against John Jérémie had been to order the dismissal of Jean-Marie Virieux, Vice President of the Court of Appeal, and of Colonel Draper.

Monsieur Virieux had refused to attend the Court on 22 June 1832 in order to install Jérémie as Attorney General in place of Prosper d'Epinay. Colonel Draper, collector of customs and holding office in the Legislative Council, had rallied the unofficial members of that Council and had voted the expulsion of Jérémie in July 1832. Sir William Nicolay also ordered the destitution of Adrien d'Epinay, unofficial member of the Legislative Council, representing Port Louis. Monsieur d'Epinay had led a violent press campaign against Jérémie. As well as the dissolution of the volunteer corps created under the authority of the former governor to help the English garrison keep order in case of a slave revolt, Sir William Nicolay announced that martial law would be proclaimed at the slightest breach of the peace.

As soon as the destitution of Monsieur Virieux, Colonel Draper and Monsieur d'Epinay became known, three other members of the Legislative Council handed in their resignation to the Governor as a sign of protest. According to the discussion that raged around me, it was obvious that the Mauritians, little inclined to accept the decisions of the head of government, were not eager to replace their compatriots on the Council – to the great embarrassment of the Governor who did not dare approach them now for fear of the sort of answers his proposals would provoke. Meanwhile, at the demand of the colonists, Monsieur Adrien d'Epinay had agreed to go to London to plead the cause of the Mauritians with the Minister.

'Perhaps all we need is to wait patiently,' said he who had been speaking about the West Indies and who gave the impression of being a man of law and order. 'Don't forget that in Saint Lucia, Jérémie pushed his case so hard that the complaints made by the inhabitants resulted in his being recalled to London.'

'Let us not forget either, my dear König,' said another, 'that Jérémie has had ample time, since he left here last year, to present things from his own point of view, and certainly to his own advantage, to the English government. So we can be sure that he will return in triumph, even if we don't see the triumph of his ideas. Moreover we've already begun to pay for our conduct of last year. The future fills me with great foreboding, I must confess.'

The political situation on the former Ile de France seemed to me as complicated as that in its homeland and later that night when I found myself on the stairs with Souville, having left the others behind on the ground floor to get on with their discussions, I realized that the management of a demesne in the colonies was by no means as straightforward as I had imagined.

V

My interview with Leperet was most pleasant. I found a man a little older than myself, charming in conversation and courteous of manner. He had taken over his father's practice, but before that he had spent two periods of time in France and England. He informed me that the inquest on the death of François had been definitively closed, that all attempts to find the murderer had been abandoned and that a verdict of murder against person or persons unknown had been filed. During the months preceding the drama two or three homes in the district had been ransacked in the absence of the owners and some pistols had disappeared. Perhaps François had surprised someone in his grounds who, on being pursued, had fired point-blank. The mystery would never be completely elucidated: one had to resign oneself to that fact.

Leperet, advised of my arrival, had prepared all the documents relating to my inheritance. When I took leave of the notary, I was truly the properietor of the demesne of Girofliers and my bank account stood at a very respectable number of piastres. I also took away with me an inventory of the furniture which the notary had drawn up for me, but I must admit that on that first day I did not bother to study it thoroughly. If I had done so, I should have been less surprised next day. I invited the notary to dine with us that evening as we took our leave of one another.

At the hotel, I found Monsieur Masse still reclining in his chaise-longue. He seemed to have recovered from the previous evening's disagreeable surprise and told me the colonists would not stand for it.

'Moreover,' he added, 'we have total confidence in our delegate. D'Epinay had already proved on the first occasion that we were made of sterner stuff. And this time he'll once again put things in their proper light. It is to him that we owe the establishment of the Legislative Council and the abolition of censorship. He's the right man to present our new appeal to the Minister.'

Monsieur Masse then asked me about my impressions of Port Louis, told me I was wrong to be leaving so quickly, and ended by saying a place had been reserved for me in Monsieur Tronche's stagecoach for the next day.

'You will have the pleasure of travelling with Madame Ghast,' he declared. 'I had called Hector and ordered him to reserve your seat when Madame Ghast, who was walking in the garden, told me she had come down to request the same service of him. It would seem that yesterday she received a note from her manager telling her he absolutely needed her advice about her new plantations. She's a great little lady, Monsieur, and a very courageous one. She could have left to join her family in France, but after the death of her husband she took the estate in hand saying it was her duty to carry on the struggle. A truly great little lady!'

I should never have confided the fact to Monsieur Masse but this news gave me great pleasure. I told myself that it would be pleasant to travel in the company of this young lady, to be of service to her in any way. It was true that until now she had managed perfectly well without my presence in her comings and goings across the island, but in every man there exists a need to watch over the fair sex, and no man could have resisted the temptation to extend his protection to this lady who seemed so exquisitely frail.

The day passed calmly. The heat was overpowering for that time of year. Souville and I made a few plans. We talked about ensuring that our visits to town coincided and he promised to come and visit my estate and give some advice. Unlike what often happens on long voyages during which friendships are made and broken with the same casual ease, the crossing had forged a bond between us that still remains intact. Whenever life seems to me empty and futile, I make my way to Pamplemousses and there on the veranda – where his grandchildren are playing and young ladies are seated in accordance with family custom – ensconced next to my old friend and listening to his serenely philosophical discourse, I find my inner balance once again. I realize then that all is not lies and dissimulation, that men and women can and will still show one another love and devotion.

When we went downstairs to join Monsieur Leperet, whose arrival had just been announced, we found him in the company of Madame Ghast and thus it was in the most natural way in the world that we were formally introduced.

'When one has known François Kerubec,' she said, 'one can only feel the greatest pleasure in meeting a member of his family.'

Her voice was nicely pitched, with a touch of hoarseness in the lower registers that was not displeasing. I expressed the delight I felt in being able to make the acquaintance of a neighbour.

'A very small neighbour,' she said. 'Only a few acres of ground, a real Cinderella beside the Marquis of Carabosse.'

'Who is lacking his Puss-in-Boots.'

'Don't worry, you'll find him on your estate. Rantanplan, your manager, is the most picturesque individual I've ever met. I never cease to admire him on horseback, with his great straw hat, his rough blue serge jerkin, his gaiters and his enormous feet in the stirrups. He watches over everything and performs wonders. The other slaves obey him without a murmur. You also have his wife, Ballet de Rosine. I expect these unlikely names must make you smile. My chambermaid, who is here with me, answers to the appellation of Queen of Carthage. It is their masters, of course, who are responsible for that.'

A sudden smile illuminated her face.

'You know, I'm really impatient to take possession of the house and get to know my servants!' I told her.

'I can understand that all too well,' she replied, 'in that I myself cannot bear to be parted too long from my home, which nevertheless is nothing in comparison with yours. I've been here two weeks, and – well, this morning I suddenly decided to return. I couldn't resist what seemed like a call from afar to which I could not remain indifferent.'

'Then I shall have the pleasure of accompanying you on your journey,' I said.

And I privately savoured the thought, feeling myself a hypocrite, but playing to perfection the role of a man to whom some good news has been announced over which he is rejoicing.

She raised her eyebrows almost imperceptibly: 'So are you not intending to extend your visit to the town? Have you already settled your business?'

I thought to myself then that I must have misunderstood Monsieur Masse when he stated that he had been intercepted by Madame Ghast as he was giving the order to Hector to reserve my seat for the journey, though she may have been out of earshot of the hotelier when he had pronounced my name. But it was of no great importance.

'I have no further business in town,' I said, 'and thanks to the efficiency of Monsieur Leperet, I've signed all my documents this very day.'

On hearing his name, Monsieur Leperet drew near, followed by Souville, and we began to talk about the festival season which was about to begin at the start of winter, in Port Louis. I had to get used to the idea of feeling cold in July and August and very hot in the month of January; I pointed this out to Madame Ghast and she replied that when one came to live on Mauritius one had to get accustomed to many new things.

'For example, you have to accept the fact that there is neither spring nor autumn here; resign yourself to the fruits of your efforts being wiped out in a few hours by a hurricane; and, if you are a lady, to suffer for six months until the new fashions arrive from Paris.'

We all four dined together, for Madame Ghast had agreed to join us at our table. The conversation was light and amusing and I remember that there was some speculation about the arrival of French actors. But when Madame Ghast had retired and we were left in male company, Monsieur Leperet thought it best to warn me about the new government policy towards the slaves.

'At first sight,' he told me, 'you might be inclined to think that the settlers are thinking only of their own interests and are absolutely opposed to emancipation; but what irritates us is the way in which such measures are imposed upon us. The government tends to elevate the status of the slave and lower that of the master. All the laws proposed seemed based on the conviction that it is impossible to be at one and the same time a colonial and an honest citizen. We would be prepared to make the concessions demanded of us if the government had confidence in us. I will not deny that certain masters do abuse their authority over their slaves, but one cannot condemn a whole community because of the bad faith of perhaps a dozen of its inhabitants. The delegates of the anti-slavery society have paid attention only to those exceptions. They have ignored those estates where the slaves are treated with humanity, just as they have doubtless failed to consider the fate of some ten thousand old people who today are still receiving their rations, medical care and clothing, as in the days when they were employable, and who would be reduced to beggary and starvation by emancipation. Not to mention the children who, from the day they are born, receive not only a complete outfitting but also their ration of rice, manioc and so on. We are not against the abolition of slavery, and indeed the slave trade itself has not existed for these last twenty years, but we consider that a period of transition is necessary. That would allow us also to make our own arrangements – for after emancipation defections would definitely take place. We are afraid that those slaves who have always lived under our protection might in their newfound liberty allow themselves to run wild, and with the help of bad examples given by certain people might foment troubles that we should be incapable of repressing, now that the government has dissolved the volunteer armed forces. Let's wait and see. On 27 June last year a new order of the Council provisionally suspended the famous emancipation decree of 2 December 1831 that Jérémie was authorized to apply on his first visit here. We have gained a breathing-space, and that's something. But as you are a new arrival in the colony, and French, you should be more circumspect than the others.'

'I've already grasped some idea of the situation,' I told Monsieur Leperet. 'Yesterday, in this very room, I listened to some very interesting discussions. It seemed to me that the new Governor is not very popular.'

'Put yourself in our place,' replied Monsieur Leperet. 'His arbitrary decisions deprive us of our best representatives in the Legislative Council. But despite everything it's impossible for him not to find ridiculous the role that certain Jérémistes – if I may be allowed the expression – have incited him to play. He thought he was disembarking in a crisis of high tragedy, and he met nothing but indifference. How will he react? It cannot be denied that he is prejudiced against the Mauritians, yet he approved the departure of Adrien d'Epinay for London. Spiteful tongues may say that in the latter's absence he won't have to fear the biting wit of his articles. Let us, for our part, act in moderation and let us not forget that in the Governor's entourage there are enemies of d'Epinay, the very ones that ambitious greed will force to side with the strongest elements. We are living through a very troubled period.'

Quite frankly, I could not see the situation in such a sombre light. For me it was a question of slavery. It was obvious that this issue, which had been raised for the first time in 1790, would have to be settled sooner or later. But since then, I've seen the departure of five of my neighbours at Grand Port, I've seen their women and children crying, I've seen the worst intentions ascribed to perfectly natural acts.

Today, calm has been restored. My neighbours have returned to their homes and all of us at Grand Port are happy at having contributed to the improvement of the lands which they had had to abandon, ploughing, sowing and harvesting them under our own supervision until their return. Times have changed since those first evenings at Port Louis. All around me, after the tempest, peace has been re-established. Jérémie has been recalled. Soon – in a matter of months – the emancipation of the slaves will be proclaimed. Commissions will be named to estimate the compensation due to each proprietor. Then the period of apprenticeship will begin. A certain number of hours of work and all overtime will be remunerated. A period of apprenticeship for the slaves and for their masters. The news was greeted without protest.

VI

Some eighteen months here! Eighteen months only! I feel very different from the carefree man I was then. It seems so long ago. Sometimes, returning from my inspections of the plantations, I find myself going straight to the mirror in the great *salon* and giving myself curious looks. An old jacket easy to wear and gradually getting baggy at the elbows, trousers worn tight-fitting at the ankles, white silk shirt, stout boots. The face is tanned, the eyes hard, and lines have appeared at the corners of my lips. I gaze at myself and tell myself that my hard apprenticeship is over and that it has marked me indelibly. I tell myself it was fated that someone in this house would have to labour and suffer, and perhaps pay the price. François did not escape that fate: neither have I. I know now that François fought and was defeated. The mysterious force that governs the world takes us all by the hand. Whether we want to or not, we just go on. Eighteen months. How very far I am now from that first stagecoach journey! That diligence which set off at dawn . . .

The great berlin had stopped at the Chaussée, at the corner of the rue de Castries, to await Madame Ghast, her chambermaid and myself. Our baggage was piled on top of the coach and covered with a tarpaulin. Souville, who had been waiting in a coach sent by his children, was to accompany us. Four passengers had already taken their places in the coach when we got in.

The stagecoach left Port Louis as the Angelus was ringing. It was drawn by four sturdy horses; their hooves rang out on the road, and there was also the jingling sound of little bells attached to their neck-harness: I remember thinking that people must be turning in their beds and falling asleep again with a sigh of relief saying, 'It's the stagecoach.' There are also certain unimportant things which remain engraved on the memory – events, thoughts, phrases overheard by accident that stay with you all your life.

It was a clear morning, the sky without a cloud. The rusty grass on the slopes of the Montagne de la Découverte rustled in the breeze. At Cassis, the shutters of the little houses along the road clattered open, pushed by impatient hands. In a courtyard, a woman throwing grain to her chickens stopped and stood motionless, her pinafore tucked up, following us with her eyes. Perhaps she had never left the outskirts of the town or perhaps, on the contrary, she had come from the south . . .

The stagecoach, with seats for ten, was carrying only seven, which allowed us plenty of room. Madame Ghast, her chambermaid and a third lady – I learned later that she was in the fashion business – occupied the rear seat with a gentleman of a certain age. The husband of the 'lady of fashion', a young man and myself occupied the second seat. Soon there began that exchange of small talk, banal and futile, that springs up between people brought together by chance and who will never meet again. But Madame Ghast and the gentleman of a certain age seemed to know one another well.

The morning passed without incident. The slopes were sometimes steep and we had to proceed at a walking pace. We passed through villages – Beau Bassin, Rose Hill. When we stopped to let the horses drink, people gathered round the coach, questioning the driver, begging him to say good-day to one or other of their relatives at Curepipe or Plaine Magnien. The big stout coachman promised to do so, proud of his importance. Doubtless he already felt himself aggrandized by his magnificient scarlet and gold livery – the gilt buttons of which were rather tarnished.

The road kept changing as we made our way towards the interior of the island. It was bordered by tall hedges and a green radiance filtered through the leaves. Rough grass grew between the tree trunks. Red berries, which I was told were wild raspberries, struck a gay note among all the verdure. Birds flew up at our approach. Sometimes there was a clearing and one caught a glimpse of a house. In a garden, children would stop playing and run towards the road. One couldn't help wondering what sort of life those who had chosen such solitude could be living. Was it from liking or necessity? Madame Ghast told me the names of several families as we passed by, but without further comment.

She had hardly spoken since leaving Port Louis. For an hour or so, leaning back in a corner of the coach, her eyes closed, she had slept, her face betraying nothing. But as we began to approach a relay station, she started to talk about the latest fashions with the other lady, who, taking advantage of the occasion, rattled on about all the items that had arrived 'direct from Paris' on the *Minerva*. These treasures, carefully packed, lay on top of the coach. Despite all the clients she had in Port Louis, Madame Rose had to remember those waiting in Mahébourg and Grand Port. The voyage was long and wearisome, but Madame Rose felt herself amply rewarded when, on visiting a family, she found herself surrounded by young beauties eager to snap up the knick-knacks she had brought them. Of course she felt entitled to ask for a few piastres more than she charged her clients in Port Louis. The journey itself cost sixteen piastres, return ticket, for herself and her husband, and Madame Ghast knew that local bed-and-breakfast accommodation was not offered free of charge. So, for example, that Italian straw bonnet, trimmed with black velvet and four artificial roses, which would suit Madame Ghast so well, would be sold almost at cost price in Port Louis, but here she would push up her price by one piastre – just one piastre, next to nothing! We arrived at the Mesnil relay without Madame Ghast having purchased the Italian straw bonnet.

The horses were allowed a breather and we got out to stretch our legs. While the *modiste*'s husband climbed on the roof, worried about their precious merchandise, and the ladies took their ease at an inn of such humble aspect that lunch there was impossible, the young man and the other traveller took a turn along the road. We introduced ourselves. The young man was going to his cousins in Beau Vallon, for the summer in Port Louis had fatigued him greatly. That was about all we could get out of him. The other fellow-traveller, Monsieur Antoine Boucard, had been to town at the request of the Colonial Committee whose members were concerned about shortages threatening the colony following the torrential March rains. The harvests had been ruined, the price of rice had shot up, and in certain shops this essential food was no longer to be found.

'In the course of all these years,' said Monsieur Boucard, 'the government, whenever there was some natural calamity, always placed at the disposal of the inhabitants stocks of emergency supplies – as a loan, of course. This time, it seemed that the government had decided otherwise. We were treated to a discourse on our lack of foresight and we were even told that it would teach us a lesson. Finally, last Monday, the town's notables were summoned to Government House and His Excellency announced that he had given his consent to the distribution of five thousand bales of rice, reserving the right to effect the distribution. But the anxiety had lasted two whole weeks. I'm still wondering if it wasn't a pretext to accuse us of starving our slaves.' These words made me realize that anxiety about the authorities' new attitude was also spreading to the countryside.

When he discovered that I was François Kerubec's cousin, Monsieur Boucard invited me to visit Pointe d'Ensy where he lived, adding that his family would be very glad to receive me. He had known François. 'Your cousin was a bit of a misanthrop. He rarely took part in what I refer to as our social gatherings; I mean dances, sailing, rambling – all the things young people adore. And yet, most of the mothers of marriageable daughters in the region had their eyes on him: a son-in-law who answered perfectly to their secret dreams for their daughters could hardly be imagined. No parents, a fine-looking gentleman, taller than you certainly, and – not to be sneezed at – a solid income and a superb estate. But you too could become their ideal, young man. I've the feeling we'll have to protect you from their scheming ways . . .'

Monsieur Boucard was the type of settler I had always imagined until now. Of a certain age, dressed very simply, disdaining neither a groaning board nor a bottle of good French wine. I learnt that he ordered his directly from Bordeaux. I took to him and promised to visit him as soon as I had settled in.

I shared some of my worries with him. 'I know it will be a hard task,' I told him. 'It will soon be one year since François passed away. I expect the slaves under the direction of only the estate manager will have been doing pretty much as they please. The notary informed me that the sugar-cane harvest had been good and that the stocks of grain had been sufficient to feed the slaves. I have no illusions. I know I shall have much to learn if I intend to make a success of the place. I'm ignorant of agriculture and I know neither the land nor the climate.'

'I can set your mind at rest immediately upon that score,' replied Monsieur Boucard. 'You'll find everything in good order on your estate. Your manager is devoted to it and he made it his duty to pursue the work already started while waiting for your arrival. As for the future, it will be a pleasure for us to offer you help. Take Madame Ghast – after the death of her husband, she finally decided to oversee her fields herself after a certain amount of hesitation. And though her revenues have not augmented, they have certainly not declined. She lives comfortably and she could well afford to treat herself to that Italian straw bonnet if she really fancied it.'

Monsieur Boucard smiled, and with the tip of his cane touched a few pink morning glories flowering by the roadside. 'A local curiosity,' he said, 'are the wild lilies that grow in watery patches and which generally all bloom at the same time. Sometimes a sheet of pink spreads through the woods and fields. It's a harbinger of rain. Next day, all the flowers are drowned.'

We retraced our steps and Monsieur Boucard pointed out to me with his cane a fairly large cottage, thatched with straw. Grass was growing in the yard and the cottage, with its closed shutters, exhaled an impression of sadness and destitution. One could see that time had begun its pitiless transformation.

'This,' said Monsieur Boucard, 'was where there lived, only a few months ago, one of the bravest followers of Surcouf, good old Dominique. When travellers happened to stroll past his door, as we are doing now, they often heard raised voices, threats and the sound of sobbing, for old Dominique, all of seventy-eight years of age, still had terrible jealous scenes with his wife who was well over sixty. One evening, at the height of a jealous rage, he killed her and cut his throat. I can never pass by this cottage without thinking of those two creatures, without wondering if perhaps they were not happy despite everything. Doubtless they were after their own fashion, and maybe more profoundly so than we imagine.'

They were waiting for us at the inn to start off again. We were to stop at Curepipe for lunch. On leaving the hamlet of Mesnil, the road once more passes through forests, with here and there a clearing and a house. Madame Ghast pointed out to me the one that had been occupied by La Pérouse* during his stay in Mauritius, and right next to it the one belonging to the Broudou family. She told me of the love story between the celebrated explorer and a Mauritian-Creole girl. A passion frowned upon by the La Pérouse family; a passion that triumphed over family

* French explorer (1741–88)

disapproval but which was not to last. After two years of life together, La Pérouse set sail and never returned.

I asked Madame Ghast: 'If La Pérouse were still living happily with his wife, would one ever mention their happiness, and would people ever think of pointing out his former house as they passed by?'

She was taken aback for a few seconds by my words, then: 'It's quite true,' she said, 'happy passions have no history.' And she remained thoughtful a long time, her face turned towards the carriage door. On the road, a light mist was rising.

VII

A surprise awaited us at Curepipe. In the inn's large dining room, places were laid and bottles of wine were out on the tables. An unusual animation reigned. The servants came running in through one door and out the other. A scullion maid appeared, sleeves rolled up, bearing a steaming bowl. Another black servant rushed to help her and they disappeared inside the house. In the courtyard the horses stamped their hooves. Finally, someone who appeared to be in charge arrived and announced that lunch would be dished up immediately. 'Kindly excuse this commotion,' he said, 'but my wife who is the very heart and soul of this establishment has been taken with the pains and I think that by tomorrow . . . anyhow, ladies and gentlemen, kindly take your seats . . .'

'Just our luck,' grumbled Monsieur Boucard.

The tired young man had blushed and turned to the window.

'Madame Cochrane is very sorry about this to-do,' the master of the house told us.

We tried to convince him that it was we who should be excusing ourselves for our intrusion at this difficult moment. He straightened his shoulders: 'Gentlemen,' he said, 'a soldier stays at his post whatever happens.'

'You've hit the nail on the head all right,' replied Monsieur Boucard. And turning towards me: 'Madame Cochrane kept the canteen for a military outpost stationed at Curepipe for several years. It has just been disbanded.'

The dishes were brought in just as Madame Rose's husband announced he was about to collapse with hunger. It was the first time they had heard him speak.

The meal was abundant and varied. Dessert arrived just as Madame Ghast asked us to excuse her. 'I must go and see that young woman before we leave,' she told us.

She entered the innkeeper's private living quarters. We were preparing to board the coach when she returned and ordered the coachman to bring down one of her bags. 'I can't go on,' she said. 'If anything happened to this young woman, I should reproach myself for it all my life. I can't leave her like this in the hands of her slaves and her husband, who, like all husbands in such a situation, is perfectly useless. I got into the bedroom just in time to prevent her from being persuaded that she should lie down on the floor in order to derive from the earth the strength needed for the delivery.'

There had been a return of that vivacity which had so surprised me the first time I had seen her in the hotel corridor, and her cheeks were flushed.

'But how will you be able to . . .' I began.

She smiled: 'My dear sir, if you had lived just one month in this colony, you would know that we are called upon frequently to give our people medical assistance. It won't be the first time I have helped at a birth. I entrust to you the Queen of Carthage, look after her for the rest of the journey. I'll return by the Saturday coach. Go on your way and *bon voyage* to you all.'

She went off without looking back. I was always to see in her this brusque and unpredictable manner of taking her leave, without any of the affectation and fuss usually associated with a woman's departure. When the horses started off again, she was already back in the house.

In fact, I was feeling a little at a loss, dissatisfied with everyone, and, as usually happens in such cases, dissatisfied with myself. I told myself that human beings have the stupid habit of doing everything to complicate their existence by taking on unnecessary tasks. Since the first visit, I have stopped twice at the inn. I bounced the new baby on my knees and in Port Louis I sought out the toy shops.

We were once more passing through dense forest where the mist was thickening and a chill damp made us shiver. Soon visibility was so bad that the assistant coachman had to get down from his seat and guide the lead horses by the bridle. We were progressing slowly and a sort of numbness invaded our limbs. On leaving Curepipe, Madame Rose had taken a pencil and account book from her reticule, but she had to give up her calculations. Leaning back against the seat, arms folded across her chest, she was dozing off. Whenever the coach bumped over a pothole, she would jerk awake and throw out her arms, but soon afterwards she would close her eyes again.

For more than two hours we proceeded thus, slowly, between walls of vegetation, and in the most complete solitude. No house, no trace of human life. The coachman pointed out to us sparrowhawks following our conveyance. Then the road started to go downhill and the mist lifted a little. As we were passing through Rose-Belle and Plaine Magnien, I felt the anguish oppressing my heart lightening somewhat. And I started thinking of this new life awaiting me, of all the pleasant things it would afford me.

My people, though they had been advised of my imminent arrival, did not know the exact date. I wondered if I should find the house in a fit state to receive me, if it would be comfortable, if I should like it.

Today, after eighteen months, I sometimes lay a hand flat against one of the walls as if I wanted to feel its heart beating. I often trace with my fingertips the pattern of the wainscoting carved on the drawing-room walls, the remarkable work of François, the third to bear that name. A gesture of taking possession – a gesture of love. But as we drove down to Mahébourg that afternoon, I could guess none of this. I could not know, and, if I had known, who knows but that I might have turned back?

The mountains of Grand Port stood out against the sky. Monsieur Boucard had identified them for me. He showed me also, as we passed by, the Beau Vallon estate and the sugar refinery at the road's edge.

We stopped to let down the anaemic young man whom I have not seen since and whose name I have forgotten. Tall trees, terebinth, teak and ebony, mingled their branches, forming a vault high above the road.

'Now we are entering your estate,' said Monsieur Boucard.

The coachman had stopped to light his lanterns. It must have been half-past six. Little haloes of radiance danced along the road. On either side, long sugar-canes bowed and swayed in the fitful breeze and they seemed to me like strange salutations. We were now advancing more quickly; the horses had broken into a trot and there was a lighter feeling in the atmosphere as night descended. We met or passed people, whose faces we could not distinguish, walking along the side of the road carrying lanterns.

Suddenly the coach stopped. The assistant coachman jumped down and opened the door. At the same time, someone I could barely see in the dark came towards me: 'Welcome master.'

'Is this . . .' I started to say, turning to Monsieur Boucard.

'Why yes, you're home now,' he told me, 'look over there . . .'

Then I noticed, on the other side of the road, a long avenue and, at the end of it, a house in which all the rooms, from ground floor to attic, were brightly lit.

I took leave of my travelling companions while the coachman and his boy were putting my luggage on the road. The stagecoach started off again and I went up to the man who was waiting for me a few yards away, with a deferential air. 'You must be Rantanplan,' I said, holding out my hand. 'How did you know I was due to arrive?'

He replied using a *patois*, which I followed with difficulty, but I was able to grasp the essence of what he said.

'We did not know for sure that you would be arriving today,' he said, 'but we've been waiting two weeks for you. All that time, when the stagecoach from Port Louis passed by, I would wait for it on the road. This evening, when I heard the coach slow down, I knew . . . It's our master, I thought to myself. Welcome master.'

The last sentence was spoken in French. I was more moved than befitted me perhaps but the good man's speech and manner touched my heart.

'I'm happy to be home at last,' I told Rantanplan. 'Is there something for dinner?'

'My wife put a chicken on the spit this afternoon just in case; she'll be making you a dessert.'

He had picked up two of my bags as he was speaking. I took the other two and we started off down the avenue. It was dark but the illuminated house at the end of the avenue glowed like an altar against the night. Shadowy forms fell across the terrace. We approached the balustraded grand stairway leading up to it. Another black appeared and took my bags. On the terrace, forming a semicircle, men on one side, women on the other, all the slaves were waiting for me.

Later I was to understand that this reception had been organized by Rantanplan. That evening, I found in the scene something almost medieval, because of the deference and servility that are commonplace in the colonies, but for which my life in France had not prepared me, and I felt somewhat at a loss. I saw that I would have to go from one to another of the slaves as Rantanplan gave me their names. Now I can manage to recognize them all, I call their children by their names, I know that they live in such and such a hut on the estate; but on that first evening I felt I was living in a fairytale. The lights from the house illuminated the terrace and in the half light those ebony faces were barely distinguishable.

When I had shaken the last horny hand – sometimes I had to seize by force the hands of these workers in my fields – Rantanplan, with a sweeping gesture, invited me to cross the threshold of my demesne.

I stop writing now and raise my head. Yes, I am accustomed to these things at present. To the great couch covered with raw *moiré* silk, to the grand pianoforte, to the deep armchairs, to the three tables of pear-wood inlaid with bronze, to the mahogany desk, to the three old prints depicting the construction of Port Louis, the battle of the *Preneuse* in the Baie du Tombeau, the Port Louis roadstead on the day of surrender. I love the softness of the great oriental carpets, and I have spent so many hours contemplating the wooden panels sculpted by François – representing scenes from *Paul et Virginie* – that I know every smallest detail in them.

The lamps with their pink marble bases illuminated, and illuminate still, my long evenings. That first evening they were burning with all their brilliance and dazzled me; as I was dazzled by the luxury of this century-old dwelling, patiently improved and beautified over the years.

'I don't know what bedroom Monsieur will choose,' said Rantanplan, 'so for tonight I've prepared the Steward's Suite. If Monsieur would kindly follow me . . .' He flung open the doors and I saw a bedchamber in the style of Louis XV.

'Did the Steward stay here in the house?' I asked offhand.

'Monsieur François used to say that it was the Royal Steward from His Majesty the King who every three or four months made a tour from Grand Port. He would come to inspect the plantations. During his tour at Grand Port he would stay in this room, and his name became associated with it.'

'I think I should very much like to spend tonight in the Steward's bedchamber,' I said. 'I should like a bath before dinner. Is it possible?'

'Nothing could be easier, Monsieur. The Steward's bedchamber has its own bathroom.'

He fetched a lighted candle from the table and opened another door.

When I had taken my bath and changed my clothes, I returned to the drawing room. Rantanplan was waiting for me.

'Dinner is ready, Monsieur.'

He backed away, lifting a heavy curtain to allow me to pass. The dining room rivalled the drawing room in splendour.

There was only one place set but it really seemed as if Rantanplan and his wife had wanted from the first moment to make me understand that I was to leave far behind me the memory of my life as a small provincial bourgeois lawyer which I had led until that night. The armchairs and seats at the table were upholstered in crimson velvet and were also of the Louis XV period. A magnificent candelabra of solid silver with eight carved branches was enthroned in the centre of the table and lit up the whole room. The plates and dishes bore the arms of the East India Company and the service of crystal wine glasses was engraved with the gold initials K/U. Gradually, as I ate, I familiarized myself with the details. Two marble consoles stood by the walls on either side of the table. At the other end of the room, between two windows that gave on to the courtyard, there was a glass case lined with red silk, much wider than it was high, containing a collection of variously-shaped baskets in cut crystal and opaline.

Arriving in an unknown house at night, after a long journey, gives one a strange impression. This house with its bronzes and glittering crystal, its plush carpets and its silence, seemed to belong to another world.

I discovered later that the sense of richness which Girofliers exhales stems chiefly from the fact that perfect harmony reigns within its walls. There is no one detail that could be considered apart from any other. And because of this harmony, on certain nights when people and beasts are sleeping all around, at a time when our actions, our thoughts, our dreams – tamed by the shadows – take on their true dimensions and their full meaning, I sense within me something soothing as if someone were taking me by the hand and laying cool fingers on my brow.

VIII

Sometimes I try, but in vain, to remember my first night at Girofliers. I only know that I awoke at the first peep of dawn. From the trees came the cries of birds I did not recognize except for the cooing of amorous woodpigeons. I also thought I could hear a running stream. It was all a mixture of somewhat confused sensations, though very pleasant ones; an impression such as one receives when, tucked away warmly in bed well out of the cold on a rainy night, one imagines the plight of those trudging down the muddy roads, water running down their backs, their feet soaked.

I spent the morning inspecting the house. Library, pantries, kitchens in the basement, bedrooms on the first floor, each with its own dressing room and lavatory and three french windows opening on the balcony running the length of the façade. Three rooms were permanently occupied by the major domo, his wife and their son. In furnishing them there had been the same patient quest for harmony, the same beauty of detail that at first sight took one's breath away.

I am in possession of all these things that others before me have collected and cherished. I take no pride in that, for I am simply their caretaker. And it may be for that reason that one day, perhaps, later . . . Life must go on, this I know.

It was after lunch, when Rantanplan came and asked me if I wanted to have him saddle a horse to make a tour of the estate, that I spoke to him about François. We were in the library, and perhaps that is the reason why it is in that room I prefer to imagine my cousin, sitting in this very armchair, beside this little pedestal table made from an old wooden capstan, or seated at the desk and noting in the family record book the last sentence he wrote in it.

Rantanplan understood me very well and as he sprinkled his *patois* with entire sentences in French, I was beginning to follow perfectly what he told me.

'I shall never stop mourning him, Monsieur. I was ten years older than he, but we grew up here together, the pair of us. He in the big house and me in the servants' quarters. I can remember how he was at every stage in his life. When he had barely learnt to walk we saw him coming down to the kitchens holding on to the stair-rail. My father was the cook and I liked to watch him at work – baking bread, turning the spits. Today, whenever I happen to pass through the kitchens and watch the motions of Joseph l'Enclume, who was apprenticed to my father, he performs the same movements exactly as my father did, and I have to raise my eyes to see if I can find again that serious little face, with his blond curls, and those little hands gripping the bars of the balustrade. Whenever the nurse went looking for Monsieur François, she was sure to find him with us below stairs, sitting on his stool and taking in everything he saw. By the age of ten he could saddle a horse and he would ride off into the woods while the priest waited in vain to give him a lesson in the presbytery. "That young rascal's afraid of nothing," the old Master would say. We were all glad to see our Master's son growing up so brave and so good-natured. See here, Monsieur, when you arrived yesterday and took my large hand, I thought to myself: at any rate, he's got the heart of our Master François. And all those who were waiting for you on the terrace thought the same thing, I know. The anxiety we'd been feeling for so long was swept away. This morning, irrigating the fields, I could hear the women singing; a song which one of them had probably just made up. A song that goes like this:

He has come, the new Master.
He has a smiling face
And his hand is strong and open.
He will give us rice,
He will give us arrack,
And our children will run happily,
And our children will run in liberty.

'. . . Yes, it was a great misfortune, Monsieur. When I didn't see him coming home for his dinner, I told the wife: "Let's wait a little longer, maybe he stopped at someone's house." I could never have imagined that he was lying over there, under the trees, and that it was all over with him. Towards midnight we put out all the lamps. The next morning I took a horse and rode all over the neighbours' lands. Nobody had seen him. As he sometimes went and had a cup of tea with Madame Ghast when he was passing by her property, I rode on over there. Nobody had seen Monsieur François and Madame Ghast had taken the stagecoach at dawn for Port Louis. I tried to tell myself that he was a bachelor and that we didn't need to worry about what he got up to, that maybe he'd scold me for having blabbed to all and sundry that he hadn't come home the night before, but it was more than I could stand. Around nine o'clock I saw l'Indolent arrive – I should tell you we call him that because he's more often kicking his heels than getting down to work – and he came running up to me. Sweat was pouring down his face. He wiped his brow on his sleeve: "Rantanplan, I'm scared . . . it was me what found him, his chest's all red with blood." So I followed him.

'You see, sir, when a thing like that happens to you, you usually have a presentiment. For the last few weeks Monsieur François had been acting strangely. He would sit at his desk for hours, arms folded, neither reading nor writing. Then he would start pacing up and down, backwards and forwards in this room or on the terrace. He who was usually so light-hearted! We would hear the gallop of his horse from afar and as soon as he came in sight of the house he would start singing. The wife would run to the pantries to prepare his lunch or his afternoon snack and he would walk in shouting that he was hungry as a hunter. Then he suddenly changed. Of course he went on seeing to all the business of the estate, but we got the feeling he was not putting his heart into it. In the afternoon, instead of taking a siesta as in the past, or receiving or visiting friends, he would take his stick and go off deep into the woods. It was from one of those long walks that he never came back home. I shall never stop mourning for him, sir. My grandfather was bought by Monsieur François' grandfather. They travelled everywhere together and my grandfather helped build this house. My father continued to serve the family and I owe everything to Monsieur François' father. He taught me to read and write, saying I should be Monsieur François' right-hand man. I was never able to read and write well but my Master could have entire confidence in me. Today I reproach myself for not watching over him as I should have done. They say it's a light-skinned black who killed him to revenge himself on the masters. And yet nobody – nobody, sir – has done as much for his slaves as Monsieur François did. There are no more prisons on the estate, no shackles, no manacles, no floggings. We were well fed: the manioc and maize were sometimes so abundant that we gave it away to neighbouring estate workers. Whenever there was something he had to reproach one of us with, he would call him in here and talk to him. He would tell the man that he wasn't an animal but a human being, and because of the way he said that, Monsieur, we'd have given our lives for him. But it was he who died.'

Later, I accompanied Rantanplan as he had suggested. In the saddle, on François' horse, I visited one part of the estate, the part that stretches down from the house to the sea. For, strangely enough, the national highway which goes to Mahébourg, passes through my territory and the avenue leading to the sea continues on the other side of the road, with the same coconut palms and mirobalanos all along it. It leads to a very fine beach. Enclaved on my territory and stretching towards the Blue Bay, is the estate of Monsieur Boucard. But I retain nothing precise from my memory of that first tour. For me boundaries meant nothing. It was only later that I learnt to stop at boundary marks. And when I see the concession deeds of 1735 and read, 'Bordered on one side by Mont Créole, on the other by the sea except for fifty feet belonging to the Company, and in a third direction as far as the stinkwood stand conceded by Charles Pierre Issecq, with the fourth direction reaching as far as the Niessen land's dry ravine, where is to be found an applewood tree,' I am able to situate the estate exactly as it was at that period, even though it has been enlarged since then in the direction of Beau-Vallon, the former Hollanders' Plain, through the annexation of the Charles Pierre Issecq concession.

As far as the Niessen land . . .

Yet another door opening towards what was to come and again I stop, I am tempted to turn back, I try to cling to the memory of the happiness I felt during the first months.

We returned home at a walking pace. The sun was going down, a green radiance filtered into the clearings and the birds were already gathering together for the night. I left the house and crossed the rustic bridge over the stream; I went to pay homage to those who preceded me. Five graves stand in a row in the shade of the great mirobolano in the Kerubecs' private cemetery, a short distance from the house. François, the first of that name in the family, and his wife, that Catherine Couessin who feared neither sun nor rain and oversaw like a man the construction of her demesne; François the second of that name, and his wife Marie Busson; François, third of that name . . .

IX

The next day, I installed myself in the Steward's bedchamber. Ballet de Rosine helped me unpack my bags and gave me to understand that she did not approve my choice. In her opinion, the Master's place was on the next floor. I felt it would be ridiculous to occupy the François II bedroom, with its communicating apartments, all in pink silk. My cousin's would doubtless have suited me, but I still did not have the courage to open François' drawers, to remove his clothes from the wardrobe, to usurp his place so brutally. I told myself that a day would come when I would finally feel accepted enough to do so.

That day has come. I tidied up François' room, put into order some papers I found: I accepted his torment. The two pages, in an envelope, are locked in the secret drawer of his desk.

> 'It's impossible for me to go on fighting like this with you and with myself. If I just stick to the facts, if I reject this fear, this doubt, this haunting suspicion, all becomes simple and easy. I'll let the months drift by, I'll let time do its work and one day the moment will come. The moment will come when this need for you that took hold of me one night shall be fulfilled. Don't tell me you didn't know I was close by, in the shadows. I shall not believe you. You had slipped out into the avenue, you went down to the beach and you knew full well that I would follow you. A woman coming out of the water, who does not know she is being watched, does not twist her hair so

provocatively. You had just arrived, in the flower of your youth. Almost ten years ago. Ten years during which I watched you living a life of your own. I told you; I told you no other woman could exist for me. And yet, at that moment, you were still inaccessible. Yes, everything would be simple and easy today, if I did not tremble at your self-assurance, if I did not have to tell myself that I must never dare question you.

The word 'self-assurance' had been crossed out, then written in again above the crossing-out. As if, after having sought for another word that would better express his thought and not having found it, François had decided, or resigned himself to using the first. I too had hesitated over that word, wanting to define its exact meaning. It has still not stopped tormenting me.

The period of adaptation was relatively brief. I sometimes managed to forget that I had spent years in a dusty provincial lawyer's office. The awakening at dawn, the calling-out of the slaves, the preparation of a daily programme and the distribution of tasks quickly became my principal preoccupations. Soon, with the aid of Rantanplan, I no longer had any difficulty in evaluating harvests. I took great pleasure in watching my slaves. Their superstitions and customs astonished and interested me – as they do to this day. Except for those who have lived near their masters since infancy, occupied with domestic tasks, the slaves working in the fields live in the camp, in straw-thatched huts. No crisis ever finds them at a loss. They appear to exist without worries, from day to day. The husband does the heavy work on the plantations, the wife does lighter jobs and the children are left in charge of an old man or woman in the camp. Missionaries endeavour to indoctrinate principles of Christian morality in the slaves. Some of them accept baptism for themselves and for their children, but others are refractory. Still under the influence of the camp's Elder who speaks to them of the Great Land of their ancestors, they become confused and hesitate. Still incapable of distinguishing good from evil, they are at the mercy of those who take upon themselves the right to dictate to them. Pulled both ways they choose just to live for the day. The times are gone when they fed themselves with gleanings from the crops and even with roots and the wild berries of the woods. Every morning Joseph l'Enclume and his assistant mix dough in the basement kitchen. Before the call to work, the slaves line up outside and receive their ration of bread. Each week they receive distributions of rice and other grains.

Yes, the period of adaptation was relatively brief. Nevertheless, from the day I arrived I had to make myself familiar with every detail so as to continue to deserve the reputation, acquired by my cousins in the past, of running a self-sufficient business; so as never to have to have recourse to others, neither to the government nor to the neighbours, in attending to all the needs of the slaves on my estate. I learnt that manioc is never harvested until after ten or eleven months, that maize requires less time, but that our orders for flour and rice depended upon the unpredictability of navigation and hurricanes.

On the advice of Monsieur Boucard, I decided to limit the cultivation of cloves and coffee in order to develop the sugar-cane plantations. Since then the canes have flourished and the tonnage of the harvest every year is above that of the preceding year. And as for the drainage works I have undertaken . . .

I still do not know how to find the courage to confront certain facts and I still refuse to call a spade a spade, so I'm like a mouse between the paws of a cat. Sometimes I think nothing has happened, that the life of the first months will continue, calm and full of promise, and then, like a sudden blow or a scratch from a claw, a word appearing from under my pen, the cry of a bird echoing the cry of another bird in the forests, the sound of the stagecoach on the road . . . it all begins again. The doubts, the regrets, remorse also – because I can be sure of nothing. Days, weeks and months pass by without my being able to obtain the slightest proof. I mean the irrefutable proof that would allow me to put it all behind me for ever, to forget, to start living my own life again. An irrefutable proof of guilt.

It sometimes happens that I am able to find again those impressions from the first days, that sort of beatitude. It seemed as if a new being was awakening within me, much more sensitive and much more sure of himself at one and the same time. I felt myself capable of great things and also of the greatest failures. I would sit down to the pianoforte and play Mozart. As my fingers wandered over the keys I could see again the life I led at Saint Nazaire. The face of my mother under the lamp. I would think of her tenderness, her gentleness, of all those simple little happinesses she had been able to devise for me. And I would think that the great love she had cherished for me had not been able to conquer that other love, since she could not resign herself to the death of my father and was deteriorating a little more each day – until the moment when I found her in her easy chair, as if she had fallen into a peaceful sleep. A love one does not take lightly, that fills an entire life.

I leaned on the balustrade of the terrace. The true lover of nature, like any other lover, knows how to admire in silence – not that his cult should thereby become less fervent and his ardour less ecstatic. In the course of my horseback tours I would ride to the extreme limit of the estate over by the slopes of Mont Créole, where the pineapples grow in their thousands quite naturally, and, reining in my steed on a slight rise, I would cast my gaze over my lands stretching down to the sea. The fields and the coppices, the trees – ebony, mirobolanos, ironwood or tamarinds – offered me inestimable gifts. When I evaluated all this wealth, I felt the blood racing in my veins. From that slight elevation, I could judge the boundaries 'reaching as far as the Niessen land's dry ravine, where is to be found an applewood tree', the boundaries to the property of Isabelle Ghast. Later, I would return frequently to that part of my estate and along the dry ravine. The first time, bareheaded, I stopped at a spot that had been indicated to me, near the ravine. Grasses crushed by some large body had begun to recover their shape. On both sides of the path, among the mingled branches, birds, reassured by my immobility, started to sing again. From the nearby ponds – those ponds which I filled in later – waterfowl flew up, to settle elsewhere.

Around me nothing had changed. If I wished, I could once again take part in social life. I could go again at dusk and tie up my horse to some hitching-post in my neighbours' grounds. I could mount the steps of their demesne and on the threshold I would find myself welcomed with the same simplicity of manners.

I have not found either the strength or the courage to do so. I keep making excuses and pretexts for refusing invitations. All day long I ride from field to field, stopping here and there to pick up a spade or a rake. Or I go for long hard rides and return at night, exhausted. After dinner I brood over the plans I have been handed, I study them carefully, I look for the best site for the installation of the steam-powered mill which will allow me to make sugar without sending it to Beau Vallon. In short, I try to live. But all I need to hear is a shutter clattering . . .

In this way the first weeks passed by. On the first Sunday I attended eight o'clock mass at the little Mahébourg chapel. Customs there are those of any small town in France. All the families from the nearby houses, as well as those of the town, gather well before the start of Mass in the little square. It is in this square, in fact in the area in front of the church, that invitations are exchanged for the coming week, where new friendships are made. No other spot lends itself so well to introductions. People discuss the news from Port Louis brought to us by stagecoach twice a week, as well as the newspaper articles against the administration.

My arrival in François' grey phaeton had aroused a murmur of curiosity. My companion during the voyage, Monsieur Boucard, hastened to come to my aid. He was accompanied by his wife and his two daughters whom on that occasion I found perfectly insignificant. I was to modify my judgement at a later date. The elder, Marie-Louise, is devout, gentle and not lacking in intelligence. The younger, Anne, has a sparkling wit and an extraordinary personality. But it was probably already too late when I met her. All it needed was a freak of fate, of a will that, without appearing to be so, proved stronger than my own. None the less, it is certain that my life could have taken a different course . . .

I'm still struggling against what I know is undeniable. I accept premeditation or reject it according to the day or the hour. I tell myself that things happened that way, one after the other, because it was written. At other times . . .

It was on that Sunday that I made the acquaintance of the local estate owners and learned the names of their demesnes – old French names, colourful and sonorous. One family came from Riche-en-Eau, another from Les Mares, a third from Ville Noire. Among the light dresses and suits there were a few uniforms, for among the five hundred men lodged at Mahébourg in vast barracks there were officers belonging to the Catholic faith.

We don't treat the English coldly, although the little square has a view of the sea and the Ile de la Passe still stands guard over the entrance to the Channel. The naval battle at Grand Port now belongs to the past. Moreover, the two enemy commanders, Willoughby and Duperré, had been tended in the same room at Jean de Robillard's place in Rivière-la-Chaux. It is twenty-three years since the English men-of-war were totally destroyed in this bay by vessels from the French navy; twenty-three years since the English fleet returned to the attack and seized the island by landing their troops on the northern coasts.

Certain realists believe that it was a necessary evil, as the island had been almost left to defend itself with nothing more than the resources left from the days of the Empire. But idealists still bemoan their fate as they see the English flag floating above the barracks. Yet we still attend social events organized by the officers there, and there have been numerous marriages between English and Mauritians. At the establishment of Monsieur Lepagnez, the former soldier and innkeeper at Mahébourg, English and Mauritians sit down together at the same table, and fraternize. It's the same at Port Louis. But certain Mauritians, among them my friend Madame Boucard, are still diehards.

It is impossible for me to think of old Madame Boucard or to speak about her without the memory of our first encounter springing to mind, on that first Sunday in Mahébourg. We were talking of this and that, the Boucard family and I, when Monsieur Boucard, suddenly taking out his timepiece, announced: 'Mother will be late.'

'You're quite mistaken,' said Anne, 'she's never late. Anyway here she comes now.'

Two sturdy slaves were bearing a palanquin across the square and as they passed by, people gave way and bowed. The blacks stopped and put down their burden. Monsieur Boucard hastened to open the door of the sedan chair and helped a little old lady to step out, all wrinkled smiles, dressed in black with long veils. Leaning on Monsieur Boucard's arm she passed close to me and stopped a few feet away.

'Here's a new face, Antoine,' she said. 'Is he an officer in mufti . . . an Englishman?'

'He's the cousin of François Kerubec, mother,' Monsieur Boucard replied. 'I was telling you about him. We travelled together.'

She bowed and came towards me.

'I knew your family well, young man,' she said. 'François II, as we called him, was my friend although he was much older than I. I can still remember his father – and his mother, Catherine, was a true settler's wife. When people smile on seeing my sedan chair, I think of Catherine. She always said she would never entrust herself to the caprices of a horse, so perhaps she has had an influence upon me. One never knows!'

She fell silent and as I expressed my pleasure in making her acquaintance she fumbled for her quizzing-glass hanging on her breast and, gazing at me curiously through it, changed her tone: 'I find you attractive. At my age I am entitled to tell you that. And I should like to meet you again.'

I replied that I had every intention of paying her a formal visit.

Her sombre little figure entered the church. It was she who was to tell me, later, point-blank, and in a most nonchalant manner: 'In every man there exist fifty possibilities in the ways of love and its attendant joys – keep that in mind, young man.'

I cannot deny that during the service my attention wandered. So many unknown faces were crowded around me that I had difficulty in controlling my thoughts. Birds, free as the air, were flying from one window to another. Among the choristers a beautiful contralto voice could be heard. Heads were bowed in great devotion, with perfect humility. My distraction invaded my prayers, when I thought that Isabelle Ghast must have returned on the Saturday stagecoach and that she was surely among the faithful.

I caught sight of her as the congregation was coming out, with her back to me, talking to the Boucard family. As soon as she saw me, I went to greet her.

'I'm happy to inform you that all went well at the inn. Madame Cochrane is the mother of a fine baby boy.'

She was animated in lively talk, and I found her incredibly youthful in her poke bonnet of plaited straw tied under the chin with a velvet ribbon; a face as youthful as those of the Boucard young ladies. I am still under the spell of the images my memory retains of that first Sunday.

Yes, those first weeks and even those first months were spent in a state of near beatitude. I just enjoyed life. I had a great ability to find happiness in the smallest things. I had got into the habit of meeting my neighbours Antoine Boucard and Isabelle Ghast frequently, seeing them not only on the neighbouring estates when I was paying courtesy visits, but also when I was inspecting those parts of my land adjoining theirs.

As well as cultivating sugar-cane, Antoine Boucard was also working six acres planted with superb ebony and colophony trees. He devoted most of his morning to work in the fields, but after lunch one was sure to find him overseeing his woodcutters or seated in a clearing linking our boundaries, in the shade of the only baobab in the south, and supervising the charcoal burning. All round him slaves would be busy setting up new kilns and bagging the charcoal they had made.

I often went to meet him. In the woods we would sit down on a tree trunk and as the axe blows rang out all around us and the woodchips went flying, as the rich scent of fresh sap rose in the overheated air, I learned from him the secrets of agriculture and animal husbandry.

Every morning Madame Ghast, under her parasol, would wander along the paths, or take a rest on a grassy slope. Beneath her gaze the slaves cleared the undergrowth, laid the cut heads of sugar-cane in the furrows or stripped the canes when the right time had come. I would provoke chance meetings and when we caught sight of one another we would wave vigorously, then exchange comments on the veering wind or the threat of rain. We would cross one another's boundaries in order to meet. We would begin to talk, passing from the weather to the harvests, from the harvests to politics, from politics to books, from books to music, and so the hours would speed away. I was astonished at the interest Isabelle took in things that were not normally in a woman's domain. I thought it was due to the fact that she had had to work for more than two years like a man. It was a remarkable faculty of adaptation that had matured her character. In public, we sometimes happened to discuss with others the subjects we had already treated at our ease under a royal guava tree or a tamarind near the ravine. Isabelle on such occasions would raise her eyes to mine and this mute complicity enchanted me.

It was not, strictly speaking, a case of love at first sight. It was rather the arousal of something I began to find indispensable and that mingled surreptitiously with the rest of my life, from the very first day we met. A door opening, a silhouette on the landing. That's all it needs.

That's all it needs. I think back to how it was. I take pleasure in assembling all the details and burning them into my memory. For one cannot keep an image in one's heart for months with impunity, nor is there freedom from danger when one begins to believe one has created in a dream a soul that is not adapted, that was never adapted, to that image.

Sometimes it happens, too, that after cruel insomnias the dawn takes me in its arms, kindly, and rocks me into dreams. Deceptively it leads me, though more and more rarely, into a world where everything becomes easy, where I can sigh with relief: 'I knew well that you would not have been able, you of all people . . .' And when that dawn respite, vanishing beneath the rising sun, withdraws its dream, it leaves me dazzled and in anguish on the threshold of a new day.

X

It is not without a certain sense of confusion that I think back to the troubled period at Grand Port. I hear again that voice with its hoarse intontations in the lower registers: 'And if I told you I got rid of it at the time of the house-searches, would you believe me?' I could not believe such a thing. If those events had not taken place, doubtless she would have found some other means and I should still be battling with my torment.

After some years, events that threw into confusion a country and its structures are limited to the consequences retained by history. Their repercussions on people or the futures of those people lose all their importance. A laconic communiqué announcing that soldiers have been the victors in a skirmish, while deploring the loss of one man, make the general public smile with satisfaction. But in the background a woman is mourning her companion, children wait in vain for his return, they are hungry and cold in a shattered home. A country can be reborn out of its ashes. The love its sons bear towards it – however discreet it might be – accomplishes the miracle. But we do not recover from glancing, sidelong blows. Paying attention to our own defence, it can happen that we wound ourselves even more cruelly. Like beasts in a cage, we pace tirelessly backwards and forwards behind the bars. All around us the cycle of the seasons continues undisturbed.

That period had begun some months before my arrival at Grand Port. I took no active part in it but it seems that we are always attracted by whatever, in some way or other, has played a part in our lives and influenced it. The events in which the inhabitants of Grand Port were involved recently reached their climax. Jérémie had been suspended from his functions as Attorney General by order of the Minister for the Colonies and took a ship for home. It is now, with the return of peace, that I am really interested in the incidents of the past month, in their political and social significance, in the efforts of the Mauritians to prove that the settlers have a greater interest in strengthening the powers that be than in weakening them.

It is only now that I take pleasure in going over in my memory the information given me through chance conversations or in response to questions uttered out of simple politeness. But the satisfaction I felt on learning of Jérémie's dismissal and seeing hopes revive of a greater liberty of action in the colony are the benchmarks by which I measure the cult I devoted to the former Ile de France.

The trouble started at Grand Port when hotheads grouped round an officer of the militia who had been demoted because of insubordination. This former officer had then declared himself openly in favour of the campaign led by Jérémie against the slave-owners. The inhabitants' exasperation against these adepts of a new order had been so great that we had nicknamed them the *matapans* – which in slave-language means werewolves. It had been decided that we would form a league against these undesirables and that we would ask waggoners and ship owners to refuse to transport their foodstuffs and merchandise. The *matapans* took advantage of this to present themselves as victims, and without doubt it was the importance they were given by these measures that aroused so much resentment among the population of Grand Port. They stopped at nothing in making improbable denunciations.

While this pins-and-needles war was going on at Grand Port, at Port Louis, after the arrival of Jérémie and his installation as Attorney General, proclamations followed one after the other. Every time the stagecoach arrived news bulletins were nailed up at the Mahébourg Tribunal. The last of these, before the arrest of our neighbours, informed the colonists that the Governor had been deceived by the apparent calm of the inhabitants, but that he had finally realized his mistake. His Excellency deplored the fact that the May proclamation had remained without effect. This proclamation commanded the settlers to give proofs of their sincerity to the government by making declarations of their arms or their stocks of armaments. As no declaration had been made to this end, we were warned that the government found itself in the painful situation of having to verify the accuracy of certain matters that had been communicated to it by persons of good faith. The result of the inquiry had been unfavourable towards the settlers. It had been established that in the colony a number of people detested the British government and were preparing an armed rising. The proclamation added that orders had been issued to arrest certain ringleaders and their accomplices and that they would be put on trial.

One August morning we learned, at one and the same moment, of the tone of the proclamation, and of the arrival at Grand Port of an examining magistrate, the Attorney Royal, the Chief Commissioner of Police and two bailiffs. One hour later, the destitution of Monsieur Regnaud – the district's Civil Commissioner – was made official and the perquisitions started among the inhabitants. At Monsieur de Robillard's a rifle was seized, while at the house of Monsieur Brodelet – who the year before had been named colonel of the Grand Port militia, an organization dissolved after the arrival of the Governor in the colony – there were found copies of circulars to the commandants of the militia and letters concerning the *matapans*, 'those imbeciles manipulated by crooks'.

No more was needed for the immediate start of an official inquiry. A warrant of arrest had been issued for Brodelet and de Robillard. Their friends Keating, Fenouillot and Grandemange were cited as accomplices; they were accused of treason and conspiracy against the government. It was even alleged that they had prepared an ambush for the regiment stationed at Mahébourg. This plot, according to the accusations, was the prelude to general rebellion with the aim of chasing the English from the colony. The accused were known for their probity and there was no doubt in our minds of their innocence. But this very certitude added to everybody's disquiet. Each one of us thought that he could one day or another be accused of high treason.

There was no perquisition in the demesne of Girofliers, nor in the house of Isabelle Ghast; but at Monsieur Boucard's the place was ransacked from cellar to attic. Monsieur Boucard's firm stance on the occasion of the interview with the Colonial Committee and the members of the government concerning food supplies had probably attracted the attention of the government. But they could find no proof against him.

The accused were taken to Port Louis where they had to stay seven months in prison waiting for the opening of their trial, despite all the petitions addressed to the Governor. In London, Adrien d'Epinay was trying to defend his five settlers, but the Minister refused to receive him, claiming that he was not the official delegate from the colony.

Nevertheless, throughout the long months that dragged on before justice was handed to our neighbours, life for each one of us continued with its personal happinesses, its fears and sorrows.

I only have to recall the evening when we learned of the acquittal of our neighbours, pronounced the previous evening, for another memory to be associated with that one: 30 March 1834 . . . The meeting at Monsieur Lepagnez's, the heavy rains during a thunderstorm, the banging of a shutter against a wall: 30 March 1834.

XI

It is difficult for me to leave the facts in their chronological order. In the family record book I inscribe dates, as did those who went before me, and opposite them the events they refer to. But from these texts there emanates a sort of desiccated air that does not please me at all. It's a family record but one that any stranger could read. 'A son born to us today, named Jean François Kerubec.'

One finds the same sentence in a different handwriting after forty-four years. The facts, no emotions. I don't want to change anything and I follow myself only the greatest concision. After François III's final phrase announcing the end of the 1831 cane harvest I inscribed the date of his decease and that of my arrival at Girofliers. I added other phrases, the yield of the 1833 harvest, my decision to increase sugar-cane production, the enlargement of the estate.

The volume, of vellum paper, gilt-edged, is richly bound in red leather. I found it on the desk in the library, offered as a lesson and an example. Witness to what had happened beneath this roof, it told me nothing and will tell me nothing concerning myself. It is fitting that only what has made the greatness of a line should be left. This admirable continuity of effort alone should be recorded. But it is fitting also that my daydreaming should lead me sometimes, out of pity, at the whim of my imagination – or of my temptation.

However I know well that the facts are there, implacable; it is no less true that I try, sometimes, to reject those I judge to be useless or embarrassing; it is no less true on certain nights, when the rain is running in the gutters or the thunder is growling, it is no less true that I try to convince myself that it is my intransigence alone that was at fault. A marvellously low voice speaks my name and an incomparable joy takes hold of me.

I had doubtless been accepted right away by the settlers because I was the Kerubec heir. I understood later that I had been privileged and that Mauritian families generally distrust those who come to settle among them. Numerous invitations followed the courtesy visits I paid to my neighbours. These country gentlemen lead a very animated social life. From time to time I joined in the frantic social round, but the quiet evenings spent with the friends I had made at the beginning pleased me more.

I would visit them after dinner. On nights of the full moon we would make up a group and go down to the beach. The girls went ahead, running barefoot on the sand. The breeze occasioned by their passage would loosen their hair-ribbons. Anne's locks, pale blonde, shone softly in the moonlight. She looked like a little elf. I was beginning to find these young ladies very charming; a sweet harmony prevailed among us and on the evenings when Isabelle came to join us I felt relaxed and happy. Happy at the thought that, when returning, led by the Queen of Carthage carrying a lantern, we would slowly walk back up the long avenue towards Girofliers and that taking the diagonal path across the fields – but so short! – I would accompany Isabelle to the flight of steps leading up to her front door.

It was on our return from one of those evening expeditions that she spoke to me for the first time about her childhood. It happened quite naturally, as did everything that occurred between us – without grand phrases and grand gestures. The tranquil course of destiny with its moments of cool freshness or scorching heat, its frankness or, perhaps, its lies.

'Just think, Nicolas, I saw the sea for the first time at Le Havre before embarking for Mauritius. The Mauritians found that unbelievable. On my arrival, when I realized the sea would really be only a few steps away, I felt an explosion of joy. I never missed any opportunity to walk down to the little creek we have just passed. I felt in me a need to run wild and sing at the top of my voice but I did not dare. I was Anne's age, eighteen, and I had come from a town where everything is dirty and sad, with grey houses lining the streets, canals full of rubbish . . .' She stopped.

Neither that night nor on the other evenings when we were together did she utter the name of the town where she had spent her childhood. I don't know where it can be. And it's too late. I've come to the conclusion that the town shelters in its grey habitations – imagination and resentment seem to tell me so – an entire race of miners or factory workers, striving to make money by their hard labour, indifferent to fatigue; puppets, for whom nothing else exists but that goal to be attained; wound-up clockwork puppets who grimly go their own way, and who stop at nothing – nothing – whose springs must be broken in order to put a stop to their senseless tread. Or perhaps it shelters people prepared to sacrifice themselves who have decided, out of love, to offer everything without demanding anything in return. I no longer know.

After she stopped speaking we walked a few steps in silence. A horseman galloped down the main road. 'I knew no other horizons,' Isabelle continued. 'The blue-striped curtain of the neighbour across the street hanging there, at the same window. It was in that town I grew up, went to school, got married. And yet I didn't leave it without a heartfelt pang. Despite the romantic picture painted of the lives of young girls, we don't confront the unknown without trepidation when we are only eighteen. I was a very bad pupil, Nicolas. When I met the one I was to marry and who had told me he owned an estate on Mauritius, I had to borrow my little cousin's atlas. I can still see myself pouring over a map, searching out that minuscule dot on the ocean, while my mother, in a hurry to get to work, scolded me. That almost invisible dot was this: this beach, this avenue, these fields, my house, your own, the Queen of Carthage . . .'

The negress walking in front of us with the lantern stopped on hearing her name. 'Go on,' her mistress cried. I seemed to detect a kind of impatience in her voice, as if Isabelle were unconsciously reproaching her for having intruded upon that inexplicable melancholy.

We often took that walk and if I started to describe all those outings I should no doubt succeed in evaluating the importance I attach to them in my thoughts because of certain words or certain gestures. Everything I try to recall forms something that, for me, seems almost tangible. One detail does not go without the other. But I'm trying also to take a detached view, to see things in perspective. I'm trying to act like someone who in the round glass of a telescope, captures one landscape after the other, examining them lengthily, savouring their beauties or coming up against their implacable aridity.

When I had taken leave of Isabelle I would walk home slowly. The sounds of revelry on Saturdays in the slaves' camp, the music of the drums and the African *bobre* accompanied my daydreams and my nonchalant happiness. I knew that in the camp, around a bonfire of dried palm leaves, men and women recreated the atmosphere of their Great Earth: Africa. I knew that they would dance, sing and drink until dawn, seized sometimes by such a frenzy that their chants were followed by total exhaustion when they collapsed and fell asleep on the earth while all round them the dancing and shouting continued.

But on the other nights a great silence reigned over the countryside. One could hear from time to time, at high tide, the sound of waves on the reefs or the call of a giant conch shell blown from some belatedly returning boat. Luminous nights and the sweet serenity of things. I would go back slowly, nothing was settled, a tacit pact was being worked out. I would mount the steps almost against my will. The house-lamps would be burning bright, as on the evening of my arrival. Every night, I would take the lighted candle in its silver candlestick from my bedchamber and make a tour. I would go from room to room putting out the lamps. But now . . . for the last few months it has been Rantanplan making the rounds upstairs. But the doors and windows remain wide open as they do during the day. Why should I seek to change what has always been the tradition? I no longer fear anything, neither witchcraft nor ambush. Nothing but what is written ever really happens.

I would go home. The house would be slipping gently into its slumbers. I would linger in the library or the drawing room. Sometimes I would hasten to return to my bedroom where, lying with arms behind my head, eyes open, I would allow myself to live for the moment. It is from that exceptional period that my true apprenticeship to silence began, my preference for solitude, my determination to protect from all prying eyes everything that caused me joy and suffering. Two or three people guessed certain things. Others perhaps had suspicions. But in the end all settles into place and time does its work.

XII

Yes, it is difficult, when one looks back over events, to follow their chronological order of events. But perhaps it would be appropriate at this point for me to speak about the stay we made at Port Louis last September, to spend a day at the races and an evening at the theatre. One year has passed since then . . .

We were discussing the project one evening at the Boucards'. The cane harvest had begun, but it was possible to absent ourselves for four or five days. It would mean hiring a private carriage to take us to Port Louis, and sending on horses in advance to the relay stations. The young people suggested the stagecoach, but the elder Madame Boucard had finally decided to accompany us, so it was planned that we should take one of the coasters that leave every day for the port with a cargo of sugar or fish, vegetables or timber. All the sugar refineries in the area own two or three such vessels. They are small lighters with two cabins on the bridge. In the bows, on a sort of between-decks accommodation, there is a place fitted up for the crew. These coasters of sixty-five to seventy tons ride the high seas very well. Some make the voyage to the Ile Bourbon. They are all anchored at the estuary of the Rivière-la-Chaux, flags flapping in the wind, waiting for waftage.

When it was settled that we should set sail on a coaster, Antoine Boucard spoke of the length of the voyage and the possibility of having to spend a night at sea, and of all the inconvenience it might cause for an elderly person – which made old Madame Boucard jump to her own defence: 'An elderly person!' she cried, 'A fossil would have received better consideration. I'm only seventy, Antoine – you seem to be forgetting that.'

In fact, apart from her phobias about horses and coaches, she keeps up with the times. She takes an interest in everything and everyone. She knows the genealogies of all the families on Mauritius. She knows that in 1730 the name of such and such a neighbour was without an apostrophe, that the name of another had not the particle he had added to the name on the grandfather's grave and that a third had changed the two parts of the surname into a single unit. 'It's a nobility with bottom,' she stated, 'while the rest are always changing seats.'

She uses a fine, biting irony which I find not displeasing. She does not spare me either, and sometimes her solid common sense, laying on the lash, can help me recover my sense of balance and offer me a way out of my difficulties.

In the course of the week that followed our discussion about the voyage, she went off to sound out the owner of Ferney. The latter immediately promised to place at her disposition his best boat, *Le Chevalier*, which was to set sail for Port Louis three days later with a full cargo of colophan timber.

On her return from Ferney, Madame Boucard stopped off at Isabelle Ghast's, then came over to Girofliers. Her slaves set down the sedan chair at one of the doors of the drawing room; it's probably from that afternoon that our mutual affection and understanding really date.

I find it extraordinary that one should always be tempted to assign a beginning to everything. I am always coming up against these boundaries. Everything has a beginning and an end and that's that. The wood pigeons nesting in the great tamarind near my window will migrate as soon as their nestlings have learnt to fly. Those wing-beats and cooings to which I have become so accustomed and which bring me back to earth so gently every morning will cease. I shall then grow accustomed to something else, I shall learn to pay attention to other things, give some other event an importance it doesn't deserve and, one day, I shall find myself associating two unconnected images and thinking: that was the period when the wood pigeons were teaching their young to fly. Or, as happened today: it was the afternoon when Madame Boucard came to acquaint me with the news that we should be leaving on the following Thursday on board *Le Chevalier*.

Her first words were uttered as a compliment: 'You've changed nothing!'

She went from one piece of furniture to the next in the drawing room. She stopped in front of a little circular table in pear-wood inlaid with bronze and possessing a multitude of drawers.

'Now this – I'll wager you don't know where this table came from?'

She gave me a look of triumphant glee at my ignorance.

'It was in Surcouf's saloon on board the *Kent*. Surcouf gave it to François II as a souvenir. I'm sure you know nothing of the history of all these objects surrounding you here. I must tell you about all these matters which I learnt from François II and his wife.'

I pushed forward an easy chair for her. She took up her quizzing glass and went on looking about her. 'Thirty-five or forty years ago, I dined here every week,' she told me. 'Life was still pretty tough in those days, we didn't have the advantages you have today. And we were a bit unsure of things, we were just groping our way. Take the indigo, for example. Every year we tried a new formula without ever getting it perfectly right and with the best will in the world we had to declare ourselves defeated. I remember one year when all the coffee crop was ruined in Grand Port. They had brought in the beans after a shower when they weren't quite dry. We had to keep an eye on everything and learn from our own experience. The slaves were truly wild. Sometimes they were disembarked clandestinely on the beaches. They had to be tamed – the word makes us smile now – then we had to teach them how to do the work and it needed infinite patience on our part if we wanted to make anything of them. After a whole day working in the fields, we looked for some kind of diversion. We would gather at one another's homes, just a small group. Two or three couples who really got on well together. We often made music. It seems to me just like yesterday. François had a pretty voice and he would sing . . . yes, you know the tune . . .' She began beating time with her little wrinkled hand and started to hum. 'Those were the good old days, young man. We made our own entertainment and in the simplest way, without ostentation.'

She lifted her chin with a knowing air. 'But that's enough nostalgia for today,' she said. 'We are embarking on *Le Chevalier* next Thursday. Both cabins will be at our disposal. The young ones will sleep in the easy chairs on the bridge if necessary. I've been to see Isabelle to let her know.'

She fell silent, seemed to be lost in thought, even closed her eyes a moment, then began to laugh softly: 'I played a good trick on Antoine. He wanted to go to Ferney to come to an arrangement with Etienne Meslé about the voyage. I let him know that I was quite capable of looking after my own affairs and making decisions. I saw Etienne myself. I'm not ill-pleased that I gave him to understand I am still to be reckoned with.'

A roguish look made her eyes sparkle. She stood up and walked towards the library. The thick carpet muffled our footsteps. On the threshold, she paused: 'This is where I saw François II for the last time,' she said. 'He was sitting in this armchair and shivering with fever. He made no bones about it. "It's all over, Herminie," he said sadly. I didn't believe him. He was only twenty years older than I and at the time I felt full of vitality. It was in 1818. Marsh fever carried him off in the end. The other François was about thirty . . .'

She suddenly stopped, entered the room and sat in an armchair. 'It's terrible, remembering them this way, those who are no more,' she went on in a lower voice. 'The other François seemed to have achieved his goal in life before he left us. He radiated happiness, one might even say ecstasy . . . I did think for a moment . . . But doubtless I was mistaken. It's another of those enigmas that I should really like to elucidate before my turn comes. It's that notorious feminine curiosity which you always have to contend with, young man. Because of it, we lend ourselves to what certain folk would call compromises. Well, we shall see what we shall see.'

She had resumed her devil-may-care manner and asked me to call Rantanplan and Ballet de Rosine. Intimidated yet flattered, they entered the library and after having given the news about their children and grandchildren to Madame, they accepted, with lowered eyes, her compliments on their upkeep of the house.

When they had withdrawn, Madame Boucard turned to me and asked: 'Have you done anything about François' clothes?'

'I've not yet had the courage to do so, Madame. But I intend to offer them to anyone who might need them and . . .'

'Did he leave any personal papers, letters, you know all the things one leaves around when one goes for a walk?'

'I don't think so. There is a desk with drawers in his bedroom, but they told me he never used it, as he was always in the library or in the drawing room on the ground floor. The keys to the desk in his bedroom are in Rantanplan's possession. I'll soon make up my mind to make an inventory. In here I found nothing but business documents. The Civil Commissioner and the notary who made the first investigations left the house as they found it. They made no comment. Their purpose was to look for the will, but, as you know, François died intestate. It is in my role of sole remaining relative that I became heir to the Kerubec Mauritian properties.'

For a few moments Madame Boucard remained motionless, her hands on the arms of the easy chair. She gazed at the great glass-fronted display cabinet which occupied a whole stretch of wall, the luxuriously bound books, the big corner sofa.

'It's a beautiful house, Nicolas,' she said. 'A truly beautiful house, and perhaps that's what explains . . .'

She ran her fingers gently along the arms of the chair, a slow movement back and forth. She looked at me and smiled. 'Nicolas, I'm an old tittle-tattle, but do listen. Put François' affairs in order. Clear up the place. You have seized the torch, carry it on – that's your duty to those members of your line who are no more. Breathe a new life into this ancient dwelling.'

I don't want to suspect her of ulterior motives, but I can never think of that recommendation she gave me without a certain uneasiness. When she decided to leave, I accompanied her on foot. A great purple cloud barred the sea and white sea-swallows were swooping low over the water. At the border of the estate, on the beach, I took leave of her and kissed the diaphanous little hand. The old lady looked me straight in the eyes as was her habit. 'I wish I could protect you, Nicolas my child,' she said gravely.

XIII

That Thursday morning there was great activity around Rivière-la-Chaux. The loading of the timber cargo had finished the evening before and Captain Buffart had nothing more to do but wait for his passengers before raising anchor. The Boucards arrived in a phaeton, Isabelle in her cabriolet with the Queen of Carthage. Madame Boucard the Elder was also accompanied by her chambermaid, an opulent negress named Baucis who leisurely followed the sedan chair on foot. Within a few minutes the baggage was on board; a rowboat ferried the passengers out to *Le Chevalier*.

Captain Buffart received us with great cordiality.

'This voyage will also be a pleasure trip for me,' he told us.

He conducted us to the two cabins, installing Madame Boucard *mère* in his own, which was the more comfortable, before going to supervise getting under way. The mountains of Grand Port silhouetted their great amphitheatre against a clear sky. Wisps of smoke spiralled up from the slave camps. Just as the mainsail was being raised, a bell rang out.

'The garrison is beginning its exercises,' said Marie-Louise.

I had already noticed her interest in the comings and goings of the military but she always took care not to betray her enthusiasm in the presence of her grandmother.

When *Le Chevalier* moved out of the estuary under full sail and entered the bay, the sailors' wives, their children, the slaves who had carried the baggage and the shippers all began running along the bank waving their hands or bits of cloth in gestures of farewell.

We beat up to windward round the Ile aux Fouquets; then at the command to 'ready about' the ship tacked about, its bow directed at the harbour channel.

We passed little boats from which fishermen greeted our passage. Some of them, figures stooped over the pole that served them as a rudder, were still exploring the coral depths for a good place to cast anchor. Others, their boats already anchored, were unwinding their lines and baiting their hooks. The latter, interrupting their labours, stood watching us pass by, waiting, it seemed, like children having some sport, to be caught up in the backwash of *Le Chevalier*'s wake.

A sort of tent was installed on the deck, a roll of sailcloth stretched between the two masts and the poop rail, and easy chairs were set out beneath it. The routines for the manoeuvres were scrupulously observed as if for a long voyage on the high seas and the watch struck eight bells.

'We can achieve nothing without discipline,' said Captain Buffart, whom I made privy to my astonishment. 'My own boatswain, an old emancipated shipmaster who used to tack all alone from the Rivière Noire to La Savanne, understood the need for rest periods, even for sailors who were still slaves. We take the command in relays, and except in emergencies, he knows I'm in charge of the vessel. He can sleep his fill.'

We had crossed the channel, and turned off the Ile de la Passe where the sandbar along the Pointe d'Esny could be seen by the naked eye only as a thin yellow ribbon. For a while my house and the Boucards' were in view, their façades gilded by the sun. The ship was making five knots, with all sails spread. There was no rolling, and only now and then, like a swimmer surfacing for breath, a slight pitching. The prow would rise, then sink again and a plume of spray would wet the bowsprit.

Madame Boucard *mère* and her daughter-in-law had taken seats in the shade of the tent. Monsieur Boucard was talking with the captain beside the helm while the girls, Isabelle and I ran from port to starboard, happy as schoolchildren on a day's outing. It takes very little for that youthful insouciance to reawaken in us. Perhaps an hour or two every day we are carefree, forgetting all the pressures upon us from our destinies. Perhaps an hour or two every day we rediscover in ourselves the full possibilities of rapturous happiness. Above the ship, high up in the sky, long-tailed tropical birds were flying in symmetrical formation.

We took luncheon on deck, without ceremony, as we passed off the coast of the Rivière Noire, with the shadow of the Morne rising imposingly behind us. When one sails from the south towards this rock, it resembles a gigantic bird of prey about to pounce, but as soon as one has skirted it, the shape is just that of an ordinary rock rising out of the sea and one looks in vain for what appeared to be, from the other side, a bird's lowered head, with its red crop and its half-folded pinions . . . I once caught two seamen awkwardly crossing themselves as they looked towards that aspect of the rock, and another nervously fingering the amulet around his neck.

At the estuary of the Rivière Noire, I began thinking of Souville and his tales of the battle between the *Preneuse* and the *Brûle-Gueule* and of how these frigates sheltered in the river while five English men-'o-war sailed by out at sea.

Five months ago, I had approached the island from this side. Now the breeze was blowing from the south-east and we had fair hopes of putting in to port before nightfall. We chatted easily about this and that – things I no longer recall. We had our siesta under the tent during the heat of the afternoon. At four bells, we were leaning on the poop rail as we luffed along the Pointe aux Caves. The sea was crashing against the cliff, a white fountain of spray rising to attack its heights. From this angle, the island displayed its most wild and tormented aspect.

Next we passed by the coastline of the Pointe aux Sables, shady with coconut palms, and when, towards five bells, we reached the mouth of the Grande Rivière Nord-Ouest, our hopes of dropping anchor before dark became a certitude.

At the port, formalities were brief, as *Le Chevalier* was coming from Grand Port only. By dinnertime, we were in the dining-room of the Hôtel Masse.

At that period of the year, almost all the settlers take some time off in the capital. Those who own houses there offer their friends hospitality, others go to the hotel, while those less favoured by fortune's riches take lodgings with shopkeepers.

It is then that the streets of Port Louis experience a strange animation. Coaches roll rapidly over the cobbles, escorted by tricorned horsemen. The coachmen wear showy liveries and the overall effect is charming. Usually, the ladies take advantage of this stay to go shopping. One sees them busy discussing the finer points of the lace at a shop on the Chaussée, compared with some other lace at an emporium in the former rue de Paris. They hurry along the pavements and on the day of our arrival in Port Louis the *Cernéen* reported that when a horse bolted through a shop window two ladies from up-country had been slightly injured. I must be fair, and add that it is not just coquetry that makes our ladies ignore or despise fatigue during their lengthy waits in the shops; it is also up to them to select and buy material with care for the clothing distributed to the slaves twice a year. I had begged my fair companions to see to everything I needed in this domain for my end-of-year clothing distribution, but I insisted on choosing myself the cloth to make a frock coat for Rantanplan. I also bought him for his New Year present a silver watch and chain. End of September. Already one year had gone by!

The next day we went to the theatre. They were playing *The Barber of Seville*, a play by Beaumarchais that I had seen already in France. There could be no comparison between the two productions but it was touching to think that French actors were performing a French play in a land conquered by the English and before an audience composed of English people and descendants of the French. I did not join in the conversation when there were discussions about the actors' technique or their voices. It was not for the theatre nor for the races I had come. I knew that already.

The theatre was packed. In the stage-boxes and the circle there were ravishing beauties, bare-shouldered in their muslin evening dresses, who were the cynosure of all eyes. At their slightest gesture their jewels flashed fire. My own feminine company rivalled them in elegance. It was the first time I had seen them decked out in formal evening finery. The young girls were looking quite serious, something quite out of keeping with their real characters, but their mother had given them so many instructions about how to behave themselves in public that they seemed petrified at the start of the proceedings. Later on, our teasing relaxed them and the tricks and quips of Figaro made them laugh till tears came to their eyes. It was the first time that Anne, my sister Anne as I call her now, had been to the theatre. The previous year she had been considered too young and she had stayed in the hotel. It gave me great pleasure to see her enjoying herself so. But the beauty of those two young ladies was still a little childish, still only a promise of what was to come. Beside them, Isabelle . . . I do not wish to linger over that image.

During that stay in Port Louis, we were friends, happy to share the same walks, the same distractions, the same meals, happy no doubt to be sleeping under the same roof. On the landing, after having taken leave of the others, we would exchange just a few simple words as we wished one another good night. A last smile, and the door was closed. In my bedroom, I would tell myself: 'She is getting ready to go to bed, she is unpinning her long hair . . .'

I would extinguish the candles in my room and go and lean on the balcony. The geraniums were exhaling their acrid little scent. A few people were still strolling in the East India Company Gardens, or walking past the hotel, their footsteps dying away in the distance. Somewhere a clock was striking. I was enveloped in a strange felicity. Then I regained my room, hastily undressed and cast myself into the depths of a tormented slumber. At dawn, the rumbling of carriages over the cobbled road and the cries of itinerant street-vendors woke me up. A new day was dawning.

XIV

The horse-races on the Champ de Mars took place on the Saturday. From noon the Chaussée was filled with people making for the rue de l'Intendance. Coaches, horsemen and pedestrians followed one another to the course. Madame Boucard *mère*, installed on the balcony with Monsieur Masse, declared she felt rejuvenated by twenty years. 'That first day, Antoine, do you remember? The ladies seemed to have been touched by temporary madness. Being able to lay bets like the men – openly – it was as if we were committing some new sin.'

Monsieur Masse had been so kind as to reserve two cabs for us and we joined in the procession. The crowds made the streets almost impassable and the direction of traffic was inadequate. This gave Monsieur Boucard a chance to inveigh against the defects of the administration. Outside the Champ de Mars, horses were pawing the ground, unable to advance. We arrived barely a quarter of an hour before the first race. Monsieur Boucard had had the excellent idea of getting a private box reserved for us a week before in order to follow the bidding. We had a box next to that of the officials, on the first floor, which allowed us to look down on the weighing-in paddock and get a good general view of the whole scene. Wooden huts had been set up on the track; they were decorated with palm leaves and bunting. The crowds swarmed around them, but there were also numerous groups of spectators round the tomb of Malartic and on the road circling the racetrack. The brightly coloured ladies' dresses stood out against the vivid green of the grass.

Street urchins had obtained a first-rate viewing stand in the branches of Monsieur de La Bourdonnais' hardwood trees.

It was a day of great carefree enjoyment. Yes, I have to admit, I take pleasure in evoking those happy hours, as if, by lingering over them, I was delaying the hours that followed, putting them off, perhaps even abolishing them entirely . . .

The Governor and his family occupied the central box, but next to it, in the front row of the officials' box, was Colonel Draper in a grey tail coat and tall hat.

We overheard certain comments: 'It seems he is about to leave for London to seek justice in his case.'

'These racecourse days, of course, are *his* days.'

'They say he took part himself when the races first started in 1814.'

'Did you know that he was a page to George III and that he served in the Royal Guard?'

'What's he been doing since his dismissal?'

As founder of the races, Colonel Draper was the guest of honour.

I met Monsieur Leperet at the betting booth. He witnessed the last race from our box; he also agreed to dine with us the next day.

I sometimes pause in front of the great tapestry panel in the library; each stitch has its particular place, each stitch has its point to make. Each point has its own importance, each shadow too. The same could be said about what is on my mind. A word seized in passing here, a gesture there, a facial expression – individually they signify nothing, and only take their place in the mosaic when they are brought to the light of day, when one scrutinizes them, links them to other words, other gestures, other facial expressions.

The day ended with the brilliant victory of Vasco, from the stables of Adrien d'Epinay. He won the first and second races, and all those around me saw in this a good omen. Monsieur Boucard felt very reassured. 'I'll tell Brodelet about this victory on Monday,' he said. 'We have to give this unfortunate man all our moral support.'

In fact, he had requested from the authorities permission to visit the accused men from Grand Port in the prison where they were being detained and he had been advised, that very morning, that permission had been granted. It had been more than a month since Monsieur Brodelet and his friends had been arrested, the judicial inquiry had been closed and the prisoners were demanding a presentation of the official indictment. Despite Jérémie's promise to do all he could to expedite the procedures, the days passed by without anything happening.

While we were discussing the fate of our neighbours, Monsieur Leperet pointed out Jérémie walking across the track with one of his greatest friends, Monsieur Reddie.

We lingered in the Champ de Mars. The procession of vehicles had started in the opposite direction. People were in just as much of a hurry to get away as they had been when hastening out to the racecourse, but now they were making more noise. The coachmen drove their horses with sharp cries and wild gestures. The pastrycooks were offering the last of their cakes and extolling their delicious taste. The sellers of slices of melon accosted passers-by. The decorations were being taken down from the booths, from where there could be heard the dull blows of hammers on wooden boxes. Shadows crept into the crevices of the mountain and on the flanks of La Découverte a small light had begun to twinkle. It was a delicious moment, but one that also seemed cruel. I experienced a strange impression, something that oppressed me like a presentiment yet that also uplifted me. Soon the racetrack was empty but for a few townsfolk lingering, as we were, to enjoy the quiet that had suddenly been restored.

We strolled down the rue du Gouvernment just as the lamps were being lit. On either side of the street families were gathering on the verandas of their fine town houses. We could hear laughter and snatches of conversation; in a courtyard, a young girl in a long frock was chasing a boy who was running away. She caught sight of us through the ironwork gate and stopped, her face covered by a charming expression of confusion. The light from the veranda made her eyes shine and we could see her bodice rising and falling in time with her panting breath. The scattered notes of a pianoforte rose towards us, at first tentatively, then giving way to a long musical phrase that trailed off into a diminuendo and was finally lost behind us. A lamp was lighted at every crossroads and seemed to invite our approach. As we came out into the Place d'Armes, we halted, surprised by the profusion of little lights dancing on the water. Lights at port and starboard, at poop and prow, lights suspended from the yards and mizzen masts. A carriage rattled past and we heard the joyful laughter of a woman. I turned instinctively towards Isabelle, and in the dusk caught that smile of hers that illuminates her entire face, and even her eyes. It was at that moment that Anne dropped her parasol and I bent down to pick it up for her.

Madame Boucard *mère* greeted us with joyful exclamations and questions. She was already acquainted with the afternoon's events even though she had not stirred from her balcony. But all the guests in the hotel had come to talk to her on their return from the Champ de Mars. Within only forty-eight hours she had made her presence felt.

In the middle of dinner, she called out to Monsieur Masse who was crossing the room: 'Let's have some music for these young people to dance to. In my time, after such a day, we would not have gone straight to bed after dinner.' All the guests applauded this idea and Monsieur Masse bowed his consent.

'A pity Leperet could not join us,' said Monsieur Boucard. And turning towards his mother: 'You must remember that young notary who came to Grand Port for the inventory of François' property, mother? He had a dinner tonight at the Turf Club, but he'll be with us tomorrow night.'

The old lady approved with a nod. We began to talk about the performance of d'Epinay's horse, discussing it with great interest, even passion, for the young ladies had wagered on it and won a few piastres. During the dessert course Madame Boucard *mère* questioned Isabelle: 'Isn't Monsieur Leperet your notary also?'

I thought I saw a momentary expression of surprise cross the young woman's features, but she replied at once: 'Yes, he has helped me a great deal with his advice and I cannot thank him enough.'

We danced until about midnight, some of the ladies sacrificing themselves to the pianoforte. That night I stayed a long time on the balcony. I knew that this stay at Port Louis had marked a milestone in my life, but I could not say precisely how.

The next day, after Mass, we discussed the possibilities of going to Pamplemousses. Every Sunday, stagecoaches transport townspeople to the Paul and Virginie Inn on the outskirts of the Jardin du Roi where stands the former country seat of Mahé de la Bourdonnais. My companions wanted to show me round this garden, in which can be found the rarest kind of spice trees as well as palms from various continents acclimatized by the careful skills of Monsieur de Céré. I was tempted by the notion of seeing my friend Souville again, but after an evening at the theatre, days spent shopping (which was still not finished) and a day spent at the races followed by dancing, Madame Boucard and her daughters begged for a day's rest.

'What milksops!' Madame Boucaud *mère* let fall acidly. 'When I think how in my young days we . . .'

She raised her ancient shoulders expressively: 'My poor boy! Poor Antoine!'

'We no longer live in colonial times, grandmamma,' retorted Anne with a touch of impatience. 'This *is* the nineteenth century, after all. We girls now have the right to coddle and cosset ourselves a little, too . . . to be ladies, purely and simply!'

'Oh, la, child!' replied the dame, 'you want everything your own sweet way. It's devoutly to be hoped that one fine day . . .' She stopped short: 'All well and good, but I know my own mind!'

She lifted her head, chin out, as was her custom when she wanted to put something (or someone) right. 'Nicolas, dear boy,' she said, arranging the fichu round her throat, 'take away from a woman of our epoch fashion, religion, diet and a goodly dose of scandalmongering and what has she left?'

Those of us who live in the company of Madame *mère* always feel out of countenance whenever she takes us to task. And once more, I was no exception to the rule. 'What has she left? As Anne has said, she is still a woman, which is after all a fine calling, don't you think?' I ventured to reply.

Through a slowly raised quizzing-glass, she lavished upon me a prolonged stare of total contempt. 'Pah! You're all alike. I must confess I cherished a higher opinion of your good judgement. A woman, a real woman, my young friend . . . but I would be squandering my precious time arguing with you at your age. It's plain to see you're taking your first steps in alien territory. The first young hussy who comes your way will just beckon to you and then twist you round her little finger.'

'Mamma,' Antoine Boucard intervened, 'our friend does not deserve such a dressing-down. And even if Jeanne and the young girls don't take offence at your opinion of modern women, I feel you are unjust to Isabelle who . . .'

A hotel guest opened the door of the little salon where we had all gathered after Mass, made his excuses and closed the door again.

Madame *mère* drew herself up in her easy chair: 'I have often wondered, Antoine, how you could be a son of mine, but I have never pondered the question with as much curiosity as now.'

She did not raise her voice, yet one sensed that she was extremely put out. Her daughter-in-law tried to pour oil on troubled waters: 'Perhaps you're a trifle fatigued, mother. Would you care to lie down for a while before dinner?'

'Fatigued?' roared the remarkable old lady. 'Look at me! Fatigued or not, I still have all my wits about me. And nothing will prevent me from . . .' She pounded the arm of the chair with her wizened little fist: '. . . but consider the matter closed!'

There was a pause. Anne got up from the sofa and leaned out of the window. A pineapple vendor was crying his wares down in the street. 'It seems funny to me, to see them selling pineapples here,' said Anne. 'Perhaps those have come from Grand Port.'

Madame Boucard appeared to have recovered her composure.

'Come and sit here beside me, Isabelle. I promised to teach you how to add a touch of frivolity to your lingerie. I remembered it this morning when I found this shuttle in one of my pockets. Look, you make a loop which you hold between thumb and forefinger . . .'

Her clever little fingers began to make to-and-fro movements. She passed the shuttle into the loop and sharply tightened the thread. Isabelle bent her head to watch and the pair of them formed a gracious little scene.

Monsieur Boucard came up to me. 'Let's go and ask Monsieur Masse if he can find some way for us to pass the time,' he said, 'at least until the fine weather returns.'

We left the salon and as soon as we were seated at a small table in the dining-room, he went on: 'Mother has been a source of some concern to me recently. She has never been especially tactful with those in the family circle, but these last few weeks she has really been going too far. The patience exhibited by my wife is worthy of our admiration. Only Anne can stand up to her and that perhaps explains the indulgence her grandmamma shows towards her.'

Other guests entered. We began talking about our approaching departure.

'Buffart will join us for dinner this evening,' said Monsieur Boucard, 'and he'll let us know if we can expect the anchor to be raised on Tuesday morning.'

The day was not as difficult as I had expected. After the usual siesta and then tea, Monsieur Boucard and his daughters, with Isabelle and myself, took a stroll in the direction of the Petite Montagne on the summit of which the construction of a fort had begun during the past week. The English flag was flying from a flagpole. 'Of what use can it possibly be?' said Monsieur Boucard as we left the rue Dauphine and turned into the rue de la Petite Montagne. 'No doubt they'll be demanding new tax payments from us and the third generation will have to go on paying it. It will be just like what happened with the church. How did you find our Saint-Louis Cathedral?'

'It's a fine building,' I answered, 'and worthy of the capital.'

'I agree with you there, but there's a snag: since 1813 when it was constructed at the request of the Marquis of Hastings, the Governor General of India who stopped over in Port Louis for a while, we have continued to pay the tax imposed upon us for its construction. That means that for twenty years we have been paying back to the government the sums of money it advanced for the building of the parish church. And we have the painful impression that we have reimbursed the cost of three cathedrals. True, they tell us that the money now serves to improve the provision of water for the townsfolk.'

The road stopped at the foot of the Petite Montagne and a footpath wound through the rough grass. Half-way up, the prospect of the town was uncommonly beautiful. We looked down upon the harbour and the roadstead where the Ile des Tonneliers stood out sharply. Towards the north, one could follow the line of beaches as far as the Baie aux Tortues, with the sea stretching in a semi-circle on which, here and there, not far from the coast, could be seen the black dots of fishing boats.

'This landscape reminds me of *Paul et Virginie*,' said Isabelle. 'You remember the passage in which Paul, on the slopes of the Montagne de la Pouce, watches the departure of the ship on which Virginie is sailing away?'

'Isabelle's coming over all sentimental,' remarked Anne.

'And what about you?' her father asked, smiling at her. 'Were you never moved to tears when reading that novel?'

'Those days are gone, papa, I know now that such grandiose sentiments do not exist.'

'What do you know about it, my poor child?'

'I only have to look about me.'

We all laughed, which did not appear to bother Anne in the slightest. Her hair, which she had put up with great care for her visit to town, lent her a sort of gravity which was given the lie by her smile and the vivacity of her movements.

'What a philosophy, Anne,' I remarked.

She did not reply and with arms raised pushed back a curl that had fallen over her brow.

'One can be only eighteen and still have a certain philosophy,' said Isabelle. 'The young have this in common – they are all of one piece, for or against. Shilly-shallyings, condescension, diplomacy come later. It seems to me that Anne is at the moment totally opposed to what we call the *fleur bleue* of romantic idealism and intends to tell us so quite frankly. Isn't that so, Anne?'

Anne suddenly bent down, picked a wild flower, then looked at Isabelle as she twirled the flower in her fingers and answered calmly: 'I like to be caught out in that way, it forces me to think twice.'

And without paying any further attention to us, she ran away and sat on a rock a little higher up.

'There's no gainsaying it,' Monsieur Boucard commented, 'that child has inherited her grandmother's character – absolutely. And I can no longer send her to bed supperless.'

'You must admit that you'd be the first to feel miserable if you did so,' said Marie-Louise.

The sun was going down. A rosy light hung over the port. We slowly began to go back down the mountain path.

XV

Every time I think back to that Sunday dinner at the Hôtel Masse, it is this dialogue that stands out in my memory:

'I have been wondering if someone could have succeeded in making her change his mind.'

'It was I who strongly advised her to be patient and to continue to work her property. Her main argument against that was that she felt herself too isolated on her land since François' death, for he was her closest neighbour. But I had just received a letter from Nicolas Kerubec announcing his imminent arrival and I spoke to her about it. She decided to give the matter further thought and finally came over to my point of view. She informed me of this decision on the very day I saw Nicholas Kerubec for the first time.'

The voices of the elder Madame Boucard and Monsieur Leperet. The faces of the elder Madame Boucard and Monsieur Leperet. A social chat no doubt, a little disconnected, a conversation by no means trivial, and in which were perhaps mingled a touch of inquisitiveness or a need to clarify certain points which appeared obscure. A conversation in which there is question of a woman who wants to leave, then decides not to leave. Why? These questions – and so many others – were ones I never happened to ask myself at a time when perhaps I should have done, because then they were of no importance to me. That very evening, towards the end of the dinner, there was talk of fishing and hunting. A predictable conversation, on an island where deer and wild bear roam the forests and where fish abound. Another banal conversation, anecdotal, but dominated by the clear voice of Anne, with its light touch of asperity, which astonished me then, but which now no longer surprises me so much. It is as if that tone of voice too was something I needed to compose and complete my mosaic: 'Isabelle, let's hear something from you now. You could teach even the most experienced fisherman a thing or two. Isabelle was not born here and yet she has no equal in finding, at night, a fish hidden among seaweed. When we go fishing with torches, it is she who brings back the biggest haul. Have you heard her talk about tides and wind directions?'

'It's because I'm a novice that I want to learn about everything,' said Isabelle with a laugh.

'And that's not all,' went on Anne, 'she also has no equal in bagging a bird in full flight and turning it into something sad and bloody. And that's something I cannot forgive her for.' She pursed her lips a little, with an expression both pert and hard.

'For our next hunting expedition in the south,' said Monsieur Leperet, 'I should like to propose the name of Madame Ghast. What do you think, Monsieur Boucard? Let's suspend judgement until we can use our guns.'

My companions devoted their last day in the capital to shopping and social visits. I was at a loose end all day. At the shop of Mr Twentyman – an English merchant recently established on the Place d'Armes – I bought a magnificent East Indies shawl. I felt embarrassed buying such a thing – something like a feeling of guilt – and my first act on arriving at the hotel was to hide the parcel at the bottom of my bag.

On Tuesday morning we boarded ship for the return. Monsieur Boucard had at first been hoping to extend our stay until the Wednesday. On Sunday evening he had found at the Hôtel Masse a brochure announcing the publication of a new daily paper intended above all to put settlers on their guard against the exaggerations of the *Cernéen*. The first issue of this newspaper, the *Mauricien*, was to appear on 2 October. Monsieur Boucard was vexed at having to leave Port Louis on the eve of the paper's first appearance. As a great admirer of Adrien d'Epinay, he deplored the fact than in his absence in London the *Cernéen* should on occasion overstep the mark. 'It will do more harm than good,' he often said.

Captain Buffart had finished loading goods for certain merchants at Grand Port and could wait no longer. The cutting of the sugar-cane had started two months before and bales of sugar from Ferney were waiting in the warehouses on the banks of the Rivière-la-Chaux. Monsieur Boucard even contemplated the possibility of letting us sail on *Le Chevalier* and staying on to take the Saturday stagecoach. But on the Monday, after his conversation with Monsieur Brodolet, he decided after all to go back with us. He had learned that Monsieur Brodelet's slaves were beginning to rejoice quite openly over their master's detention. Although his passion for politics made me smile, I could not help admiring such patriotism, for every day we were made increasingly aware of the gravity of the situation. We knew that once again the island of Mauritius was reaching a decisive turning point in its history and that it required the vigilance of all its children.

However, to console himself for having to wait until Saturday to receive the first number of the *Mauricien* by stagecoach, Monsieur Boucard insisted on going to congratulate Monsieur Eugène Leclézio, the founder of the new periodical, on the moderate tone of his prospectus. Which obliged us to raise anchor two hours late.

Quite unjustly, the captain accused Monsieur Boucard of being responsible for the unfavourable winds. 'A sailing should never be delayed,' he grumbled as he paced the deck, his old pipe gripped between his teeth, 'that's just asking for trouble.'

'Don't be so superstitious, Buffart,' said Monsieur Boucard, much amused. 'Two hours early or two hours late, the course to Grand Port will always be the same and the direction of the wind . . .'

'If you were a seaman, I'd have you keel-hauled to teach you a lesson and make you respect our regulations. That's right, our regulations, and not our superstitions as you claim!'

'The worst that could happen,' broke in Anne, 'would be if we had to spend the night on the bridge. Which would not be all that unpleasant, captain.'

The captain's displeasure, more feigned than real, gradually died away. In the afternoon, the two friends, seated facing one another, were playing an interminable game of chess.

We spent the night in the armchairs, under the radiance of a huge round moon that appeared to move across the heavens absentmindedly and to be charged with malevolent presages. And yet, that night, night of happiness, was all warmth and innocence. Stretched out in her armchair, Isabelle, with raised arm, pointed out the principal stars and told us their names.

XVI

It was with a sense of indescribable pleasure that I returned to my own house. I no longer tried to suppress the feelings that were growing in my heart. Did I ever think of protecting myself against them? The pleasure of being back home again was linked to the pleasure of resuming my intimacy with Isabelle. The six days we had spent together, but in the company of others, had deprived us of our meetings in the fields and of our after-dinner walks. Those six days had forced us to wear a mask that was beginning to feel irksome.

For the first time, on that Wednesday in October, as I made the round of the oil lamps before going to bed, I thought about the future. In the rose-silken bedchamber, I paused in front of the *semainier** of mottled mahogany, ornamented with bronzes of ancient Roman inspiration, in front of the mirror which seemed suspended between two amoretti, in front of the great canopied four-poster, immense among its hangings of rose silk. Each week, according to tradition, the bed is given fresh sheets under its satin counterpane by the ministrations of Ballet de Rosine. This October Wednesday, I told myself that one day the East Indies shawl would rest in one of the drawers of the *semainier*. I know today that the shawl has crossed the oceans, but where is it now?

Life went on. The conversation Monsieur Boucard had had with the

* A small bureau with seven drawers, each originally intended to hold a razor, one for each day of the week (*semaine*)

Grand Port accused impelled us to deepen our concern for their estates and their slaves, a task that considerably diminished our leisure time, even though everyone lent a hand. At Port Louis, the dissolution of the Colonial Committee had been decided by the Governor, and Jérémie, doing his utmost to gain time, spared neither judges nor the accused. He was hoping to replace the three judges of the Supreme Court by three others who would support him in every way.

Once the cane-cutting was over, I threw myself into the clearing of a few neglected fields where I had useless indigo plants uprooted.

The weeks went by. In December, a great gale of insubordination blew through Grand Port. At Monsieur Brodelet's, over-enthusiastic demonstrations among the slaves had to be suppressed. We were doubtless a hair's breadth from revolution. Each camp had its *séga*. At Monsieur Boucard's they had one singing the praises of Jérémie's elegance without ever having set eyes on him:

Missié Zérémie fine arrivé
Capeau coco sir l'côté.
Son habit larze' galonné
Tou les samedis dans séga . . .

Mister Jérémie's arrived
With his hat on one side.
His jacket is all laced with gold
Every Saturday in the *séga* . . .

It often happened that drumbeats could be heard at night from one estate to the other; a strange dialogue, a sort of onomatopoea, slow at first, then more and more frenzied. On certain nights, I stood leaning on the balustrade of my terrace for a long time. The sea, invisible in the darkness but not far away, exhaled its acrid smell of iodine and dried seaweed. In between the performances, when one drum had fallen silent and another on the mountain slopes or away beyond the Hollanders' Plain had not yet begun to transmit a reply to the message, I could hear dropping to the ground the broad, autumnal leaves of the mirobolanos. Silence would weigh heavily for five or ten minutes, then the rhythmic sounds would begin again and one was gripped by a sort of irrational anxiety.

One night I called in Rantanplan: 'What does the drumming mean?'

I could see he was torn between loyalty towards his people and the duty he owed to those who slept beyond the stream, as well as to myself. He hesitated and a strange light flashed from his eyes: 'They say the time has come, Monsieur.'

But while other proprietors lived in constant fear, I benefited from the humanity my cousins had always shown towards their slaves.

At Isabelle Ghast's, her manager became insolent and increasingly intractable. One night, towards the New Year, I watched Isabelle approaching, unaccompanied and pale, and I decided on immediate action if it was advised.

'I no longer know what I should do. I'm no coward, but . . .'

She was no coward, I knew that. She would roam around her estate at all hours and had done so ever since her arrival in the colony, with or without the company of the Queen of Carthage. The next day, I spoke to Monsieur Boucard about her difficulties. We considered them dispassionately and it seemed to us that the wisest solution would be to advise Isabelle to dismiss her manager and emancipate her slaves. This was done, and on her estate calm was gradually re-established.

On 2 January, I organized a party for the distribution of clothes and small presents to my workers. Rantanplan showed a boyish delight when I handed him his watch and chain, and from that day on, we never saw him without the big chain looped across his chest, attached to the buttonhole of his frock coat, with the watch safely tucked away in a little cloth bag in his pocket.

The Boucards and Isabelle had accepted my invitation to the party and agreed to help me arrange it. The evening before I had taken Isabelle the East Indies shawl. She had placed it over her shoulders, and when she arrived told me simply: 'This is by way of thanks.'

After the good wishes of my employees as they lined up to greet me, saying: 'May you always remain as you are now', I asked my friends to stay on for dinner. Madame Boucard *mère* presided over the meal. It was a very animated evening. The candles were lit in all the wall-sconces, the crystal glasses and the silverware glittered on the table. For the dessert, Rantanplan provided us with a great surprise: a magnificent set piece depicting the cabin of Paul and Virginie made of nougat and stuffed with crystallized grapefruit and tomatoes. Anne refused to let us touch it.

Yes, I remember it as a dinner marked by lively conversation. Not just because it was the first time I was receiving my friends for dinner, not just because it was the first time Isabelle had sat down to my table, but because of the strange atmosphere of those festive days when one tells oneself that the good wishes one accepts so nonchalantly could – indeed should – become realities. I was bound by a delicious, tacit agreement. Not a word had been spoken, and yet I knew that I had made my choice forever, despite something still keeping me back. I discovered everything a profound love can arouse. Those childish moods, those useless worries, that unconscious jealousy, those sudden flare-ups, those strange caprices and that feeling of being overwhelmed by a look or a smile. I felt the need to make the sweet euphoria into which I was sinking last as long as possible.

In the same month, a cyclone hit the island, roughing up our plantations but not causing as much damage as at Port Louis where there were also floods. The two bridges across the Grande Rivière Nord-Ouest were carried away. Streams overflowed their banks near the gardens of the East India Company and a woman died by drowning. A prisoner in my house, I watched trees being split open and their foliage wrecked as I stood at the window. The sea was an angry colour. The houses seemed to be bracing themselves against attack. The storm lasted twenty-four hours. The next morning, the landscape was devastated and the avenue was littered with shredded branches and leaves.

The days raced by. I went on meeting Isabelle after dinner – at the Boucards', with the Queen of Carthage, or in the avenue of Girofliers where she would pace up and down slowly. Only once did she pluck up the courage and enter the house. It was the evening when she sought help and advice about her manager. Only once – and then that other, that second time – the one I still cannot remember without emotion.

XVII

It was in February, during one of those after-dinner encounters, after the manager had been dismissed, that Isabelle let me know of her wish to sell her estate. 'I've come to the conclusion that I can't go on working as I've been doing so long. The perpetual terrors of the past weeks, the responsibilities, the decisions to be made, it has all become too much for me to bear. I have been thinking it over, and the best thing for me to do would be to carry out the project I had formed before: sell the property and, investing the money obtained from the sale, go and live elsewhere or return to France.

Nothing had prepared me for such news. I could not accept it. I could not agree with Isabelle's ideas. I did not understand how she could be so disenchanted. Weary of waking up each day at dawn, weary of mapping out a schedule of work each day, weary of worrying that expenses could be higher than income. I could not accept the sight of her discouragement when I admired her pride and her tenacity so much. I told her so. She looked up at me with a face that the pallid light of the moon made even more pathetic. 'Believe me, Nicolas, it would be for the best that way. Only, you see, I thought . . . It seems to me that course would be the least painful . . . I don't know if it will be possible, but it would be less hard for me if it was a friend who bought my estate.'

'Isabelle,' I cried, 'you've just given me a marvellous idea. I shall buy your estate and you shall be my manager.'

She made a gesture of protest, but I caught her hands in mine: 'Listen, you'll continue to look after the plantations and to instruct the slaves. You will carry out my orders and I'll share the proceeds with you.'

She tried to release her hands, but I was holding them tightly in mine. They felt soft and cold, a little shaky, and I tried to warm them.

'You will continue to live in your house. You will still be able to walk around the fields, and I shall not be looking in vain for your parasol moving along the paths. And what about our evenings together, Isabelle? Had you thought that we could no longer enjoy the pleasure of meeting this way, and have you accepted that?'

She did not answer immediately. It seemed as if she was pondering something in her heart, that she was fighting against something. Minutes went by. Finally she looked up at me again. 'Life isn't always easy, Nicolas.'

I bent my head. Her hands had a scent of flowers. But before Isabelle could pull them away from me I had felt them trembling under my lips.

We began to walk along the road leading to her demesne. Silently. We were side by side and sometimes my arm brushed against hers. At the bottom of the steps, I bade her good-night. She held my hand a long time, then rose on tiptoe and and kissed me on the cheek, in a sisterly way, as if to thank me. I stood taken aback as she mounted the steps.

When I got home, I lingered in the drawing-room. I went to the liquor cabinet and poured myself a glass of gin. Mentally, I was behaving like a boy who has been given the chance to realize a dream. The idea of being able to come to Isabelle's aid, without needing to change our habits, filled me with exaltation. Although I had sensed in her a certain reticence, I did not doubt that I should obtain her consent. I felt annoyed with myself for not having guessed, underneath her courageous stance, that weariness she had just revealed to me along with her financial worries. I promised myself that I would offer her a price higher than the one she had fixed upon, and I also thought I might have her house repaired and redecorated.

The very next day I was eager to take action. So as not to look as if we had been making secret plans and thus attract attention, I had decided to make Monsieur Boucard privy to my intentions, telling myself that the authority of his voice could put things right if some ill-willed person should venture to pass comments on the purchase. I went to see him in the morning.

I had them saddle Taglioni, the little bay mare I had bought in

January. It was almost the end of summer. The sugar-canes were already tall in the fields – except those planted this year on new ground – and the view was less extensive. All the same there were glimpses of the sea here and there. I entered the avenue. On the national highway, I stopped to let the Mahébourg garrison march past. It was going in the direction of Beau Vallon. The soldiers were singing and rhythming with their footsteps the incomprehensible words. I found myself trying to copy one of the phrases under my breath and my accent made me smile. They marched away and I crossed the highway, into the second section of the avenue. Along the edge, behind the coconut palms, the frangipanis were bursting into bloom. I was feeling light-headed and explained it by the excess of light and colour all around me.

The mare was proceeding at a walk. When I drew near the path leading to the Boucard estate, I heard the screeching sound of saws cutting into tree trunks. Soon I entered the clearing where the woodcutters were working. I was pleasantly surprised to find Monsieur Boucard there for I thought I should have to go and look for him in the fields. When he saw me he came to meet me and after I had dismounted I tethered the mare to the branch of a young ebony tree.

All through the previous evening, and during the first hours of the morning, I had been telling myself that the situation was clear-cut: Isabelle was selling her estate and I was purchasing it. But when I found myself in the presence of my friend, I felt embarrassed. The very fact of not being able to speak about this project to him without embarrassment clearly indicated that there was something about this transaction that would cause surprise when it became known that Isabelle would continue to occupy her house and supervise her slaves. However, I could not accept any other solution and I did not want Isabelle to accept any other either. But what had seemed to me so clear-cut one hour ago as I was riding quietly down the avenue on Taglioni now appeared to me insurmountably complicated when I found Monsieur Boucard's sharp eyes scrutinizing me.

As usual, we sat down on a felled tree trunk, away from the woodcutters. I did not know how to approach the question and doubtless my rather restrained behaviour was noticed by my friend, because after an exchange of the usual greetings he asked: 'Is there something bothering you, Nicolas?'

I took quick advantage of this lead, carefully choosing every word I spoke: 'It's like this: I saw Isabelle yesterday and she spoke to me of her wish to sell her estate, and I'm thinking I would do well to purchase it from her.'

Once I had spoken out, I felt relieved, and I thought all that was needed now was the use of a little diplomacy to bring my plan to fruition. I stopped playing with the little branch of eucalyptus I had picked up as I sat down, to put myself in countenance, and looked at Antoine Boucard. He had crossed his hands on top of his walking stick and leaned his chin on them. A pair of turtle doves flew through the clearing.

'It wouldn't be such a bad move,' he said finally. 'But I don't quite understand . . . Did she tell you the reason for this decision?'

'As I understood it, the costs were becoming too high for her.'

He turned towards me: 'Too high?' he repeated.

He seemed to want to add something, then changed his mind, so I went on: 'She's probably tired also . . .'

I did not feel inclined to stress this last point. The first seemed to me to be sufficiently persuasive. One does not always have much confidence in the administrative abilities of a woman. The business with the manager had shown us that despite all her firmness of character there were difficulties that a woman could not overcome without a man's help.

'Excuse my surprise,' said Monsieur Boucard, 'but nothing had prepared me for the news that Isabelle should once again have taken up this sale project. I just can't explain it . . .'

He paused once more. Today I can understand what he was thinking, and in the circumstances I believe he gave proof of great tact. If he had unburdened himself to me then and there, I should probably never have believed him and never have accepted his arguments.

'Did she tell you she would be leaving the colony?' he asked.

Again, I felt embarrassed, but he was not looking at me. I told him that Isabelle had made vague allusions to her possible departure and I followed this up with the announcement of my intention to ask her to go on supervising her plantations for the next few months.

'If she has really decided to sell, you'd make an excellent deal, better perhaps than you expected,' Monsieur Boucard concluded.

He smiled. I thought he was being ironic. I know now that if he was, it was certainly not in the way I believed.

The woodcutters were sawing up an enormous eucalyptus trunk. At each movement of the saw, a fine dust was thrown out of the timber, which lay upon a wooden support, and was piling up on the ground. The birds, familiar inhabitants of the clearing, kept hopping from branch to branch and preening their feathers with their sharp beaks. Still feeling ill at ease in body and in thought, confronted by a man of whose judgement I was in awe, I postponed my departure. I had a hard time for the next quarter of an hour talking about other matters such as irrigation and manure.

I went home for luncheon. The big rusty red leaves of the mirobolanos kept spiralling down round my head. Gently carried by the breeze, they lay scattered across the lawns; standing out against the green of the grass they looked like motionless flames.

At Isabelle's, the path leading to her house had been bordered by a sort of plant whose twisted branches produced flowers resembling huge hands with long, slender petals like fingers. These crimson and pink flowers formed a kind of vault. It had taken three days' work by three men to root up this border and another three days to plant young palms in their place. The whole perspective had been modified – I'm not sure if it was for the better.

Rantanplan led Taglioni to the stables while I went to wash. During the meal, I sent for Ballet de Rosine to compliment her on the dish of paradise fish she had prepared for me.

'I really think,' I told her, 'that the paradise fish Mark Antony brought at great expense from Asia to make a banquet for Cleopatra could not have tasted as good as those you served me.' She curtseyed with a delighted smile. After that she announced to all and sundry that her cooking was better than that of Monsieur Antoine Boucard's cook, and that it was Monsieur Nicolas who had told her so.

After luncheon, I wrote to my old friend Souville and to Monsieur Leperet, inviting them both to come and spend a few days at Girofliers. I had Taglioni brought out again and rode her to Mahébourg to catch the first stagecoach leaving for Port Louis. I strolled around the streets of Mahébourg, making a stop at the library. At Monsieur Monvoisin's I bought a little ebony casket inlaid with mother of pearl, and there met Etienne Meslé, the owner of Ferney, who had returned from Port Louis the evening before. He gave me the latest news from the capital and about our neighbours. In the course of the previous weeks, John Jérémie had finally overstepped the mark. He had not hesitated to levy formal accusations against the Supreme Court judges, charging them with abuse of authority and complicity in the deeds blamed upon the settlers of Grand Port. The Governor had come to realize that he could not support Jérémie's demands without compromising his own position. Especially as he saw him challenging the competence of the judges, for Jérémie was insisting that these judges would be capable of partiality in the trial of the settlers. Etienne Meslé thought that the trial process was now well under way and that things would suffer no further delay.

We parted and I went to take tea at Monsieur Lepagnez's inn. I stayed there quite a while, listening for perhaps the tenth time to his account of the battle of Grand Port. '. . . I could have watched it from my window. Witnesses of the battle told me that the *Magicienne* was right there when she blew up. Just where that fishing boat is lying now . . .' Corseted in his frock coat, the old soldier pointed a withered finger towards the bay. I kept nodding, seeming prodigiously interested but actually thinking of other things. All in all, I was just killing time and I was longing for nightfall.

But night came and I was still waiting in vain. From the terrace I could see no shadowy figure coming across the diagonal field-path. I walked down the avenue to the shore but met no one. Little pouncing waves wetted the sand. From time to time a fish jumped and a slight splash was heard.

At eleven o'clock I decided to go to bed. I was at a loss. An impenetrable silence enveloped the house. I slipped between the sheets perfumed with *vetiver* and spent an appalling night. I dreamed that I was wandering over an immense plain looking for someone of whom I knew nothing at all. Then the landscape changed and I found myself on the edge of an abyss, clinging to a crumbling ledge. I fell with a shriek and awoke with a forehead bathed in sweat, hands chilled and a heart racing with big heavy beats. I lit a candle and started to read. When a pale gleam began to show in the east, I extinguished the candle and fell into a heavy slumber.

The two following days were days of fruitless waiting. On the third, I decided to get a book Isabelle and I had been discussing and send it to her with a message. Thus I knew that she was not ill, for my messenger found her on the threshold of the former indigo factory which she was transforming into a granary. That third day seemed to me longer than the preceding ones. When I had drunk my after-dinner coffee, I went down the steps in front of my house. I had decided to go to Isabelle's that very night if she did not come to me; but scarcely had I gone a few steps when I recognized her figure coming across the diagonal field-path. She was proceeding unhurriedly through the dark, and when we met I could no longer control myself: 'You've made me spend three days in torment,' I told her, 'just when we both had decisions to make.'

She laughed and replied: 'You get carried away for very little, Nicolas. I wanted to leave you time to study the proposal. I was afraid of influencing your decision unconsciously by my presence. But this afternoon as I was going to Mahébourg I met Monsieur Boucard. He told me you had made your decision and so I've come . . .'

'Have you decided to accept my conditions?'

We took the way back to Girofliers. Through the trees, we could see the lights of the house shining, and when we reached the avenue we stopped for a moment. The breeze, passing through the open windows, made the curtains wave languorously.

'Your conditions are such, I could hope for nothing better,' Isabelle replied, as we started down the avenue towards the sea. 'You offer me the possibility of staying on in the house I have lived in since my arrival here, amid these fields that with my own eyes I saw being gradually cleared from the bush. I told you how greatly attached I am to these things. Abandoning everything that has been my reason for being here would have required such an uprooting that I could not have borne to settle elsewhere on the island of Mauritius: I should have been compelled to return to France. I thank you for having thought of this solution which, while relieving me of anxiety, will allow me to go on tending these fields I love, and to feel myself of some use still.'

Just when I thought our relations had reached a point of intimacy outside my grasp during the previous months, I realized that I must be circumspect and handle Isabelle's sensitive soul with kid gloves. She would have to feel really useful, indeed indispensable during the first months. Afterwards . . .

'I've started a few repairs which I expect to finish within three weeks or a month.'

'Forget the repairs, Isabelle. It seems to me we should talk about other things now,' I broke in nervously.

She stood still.

'How highly strung you are, Nicolas!' she said.

'I'm not a drawing-room ornament,' I growled.

'All the more reason to talk business. The estimate I received for the work . . .'

When I left her, we had arranged that Monsieur Leperet would draw up the sale contract during his stay at Girofliers.

XVII

The following week was devoted to the maize harvest at Girofliers. 'One of our best harvests,' Rantanplan said as he watched the carts loaded with ears of corn being pulled along by bulls. We tie the ears in bunches by the leafy sheaths and then suspend them for drying in open sheds. After a few weeks, the ears are shelled and the grains are stored until it is time to mill them for consumption.

But my mind was far away from all that! I was living in a world apart, where I was alone, and where I felt happy. Isabelle was a little distant: I had got used to that. I told myself that the surrendering of her estate would not be without difficulties for her, that any other stance would have surprised me as seeming unworthy of her. I felt rather inclined to show patience and indulgence towards her. I was content to wait.

Letters from Souville and Leperet announced their arrival for Saturday 1 March. I decided to give the François II bedchamber to Souville and the François III to Lepéret. Wardrobes and drawers were empty in the bedroom that had once belonged to my older cousin, the second to bear the name of François. His son had had the painful task of clearing up the place, but I had still not brought myself to get rid of the latter's own clothes. It was the first time I had felt tempted to do so, but I resisted the temptation. I did not want to appear to be chasing his shade from a room where he had spent all his life, simply in order to offer it to a stranger. I contented myself with having a chest brought up which we never used and in which Leperet could put his clothes.

All the furniture on the first floor was locked up and Rantanplan had charge of the keys. I asked him for them. He used the occasion to reproach me for not occupying the bedchamber I was entitled to, that of François II.

'I made the same complaint to Monsieur François and at first he told me he would occupy it when he got married, adding that this was not very likely. But a few months before his death, he seemed to have been considering the idea of marriage, for he said: "Just a little longer, Rantanplan, give me time . . ."'

On the Saturday, I waited for my friends on the national highway. They had had an excellent journey.

'But we're glad to have reached our destination,' said Souville, 'especially since we began to feel the old rheumatism playing us up as we passed through Curepipe.'

They were both in high spirits. Rantanplan and one of his sons, Cupidon, had come to escort us, and that first arrival of mine, at night, was vividly brought back to mind.

'I was badly in need of a holiday, and your invitation came just at the right time,' said Leperet.

'I must warn you that I've work for you.'

He gave me a questioning look.

'We'll have plenty of time to discuss it,' I told him.

'I can only give you a week,' said Souville. 'I shall take the stagecoach on Thursday or Friday. Tronche still does not know exactly on which day he will leave Mahébourg.'

'I am in no hurry,' said Leperet.

I conducted them to their rooms and Rantanplan prepared the baths. I knew from experience that after such a journey one was glad to wash away the dust of the roads.

The announcement that dinner was ready found us gathered around the old capstan table, glasses in hand. For the first time since my arrival, it seemed to me that the library was recovering something of the atmosphere for which it had been created. A reunion of joyous companions unafraid of the brandy bottle and talking with complete frankness as they sat ensconced in their easy chairs, their feet up on footstools. I felt I was experiencing one of those occasions from former times, convivial evenings during the early years, when there were only five or six slaves on each estate and the masters had to wield the saw and the hammer, the pickaxe and the spade. When night fell, they must have assembled here to talk about their home towns, to exchange impressions, to confide their hopes and their disappointments. Crouched at their feet, with little regard for the plushy carpets, the dogs must have rested, muzzle between forepaws. And the women, accustomed to their harsh life, probably distributed wineglasses and jugs of wine, not taking offence at the coarse speech and frank jokes of the men.

The second generation, according to what old Madame Boucard had told me, led an easier life and were more refined. And here we were, belonging to the third generation united in this very room, quaffing our wine and telling *risqué* stories, just enjoying ourselves. I had the pleasant conviction that all was well thus, that my guests, at ease, did not treat me as a host but as their friend.

Souville was beginning some hunting anecdote or other when Rantanplan, lifting the great curtain of golden silk, announced that dinner was served.

On the threshold of the dining-room, the former seagoing captain expressed his amazement and admiration at the sight with a single word: 'Zounds!'

The glasses and the silverware were gleaming. Rantanplan bore in the steaming soup tureen. We took our seats.

The next day, before and after Mass, my guests met numerous friends on the little square in front of the church. We took a constitutional round the place before luncheon and went to inspect the works being carried out over by the ponds. In the course of the preceding two weeks, a marsh had been drained dry and they had started to fill it in. I had thought it pointless to waste such an important area of land when two or three months of work would be enough to turn it into a cultivable field. The disappearance of the ponds would remove from this corner of the estate its rich verdure, its shade and its coolness. I had promised myself not to touch the path where François's body had been discovered, but to make the place into a small copse, an oasis in the middle of the fields.

In the afternoon, we got ready to honour the invitation given us by the Boucards. While we were waiting for Souville who was busy in his room, I let Leperet know about my project. At first he listened in silence, then brusquely he asked if I had just taken this decision and whether the offer had been initiated by Isabelle or by me. I related some of our conversation and as he listened he kept nodding his head. When I fell silent, awaiting his advice, he told me that as he was also Isabelle's notary he would prefer to have a talk with his client before delivering his opinion. Evidently Isabelle, whom he had greeted at the church, and with whom he had exchanged a few words in our presence, had not had time to speak to him about the sale. Meanwhile Souville joined us and we set off.

It was Madame Boucard *mère* who welcomed us in the courtyard. Using an enormous pair of scissors, she was pruning the roses in the garden. She had made a great impression on Souville when she arrived for Mass in her sedan chair. He thought her an eccentric character.

'I was just saying this morning that we never see you now, Nicolas.'

I did not respond. She shook her skirt to rid it of the severed stalks that had clung to it.

'I had more or less adopted him and when I don't see him for several days I wonder if he has done something silly,' she told Souville who was walking beside her.

We were walking towards the house when Marie-Louise and Anne came running out as was their custom. 'Girls, girls!' said their grandmamma, 'try to behave like young ladies. We'll never tame them,' she added, turning to us. 'They're little savages.'

'I'm glad to hear it,' said Souville. 'Life will start soon enough to put some gravity on their young faces. Let's not spoil it for them now. Ladies, an old seadog lays his homage at your charming little feet.' He had adopted a ceremonious and at the same time comical air, and the girls could not help laughing.

'You resemble our uncle the captain whose portrait is in the dining-room,' said Anne. 'And as I've grown up under his gaze and as I often have long talks with him, I wonder if I shouldn't give you a kiss!'

With a dainty hand poised on Souville's shoulder, she stood on tiptoe. 'Anne!' the grandmother scolded, laughingly.

But I could see that she had won over the old sea captain instantly. Marie-Louise, much calmer, stood near Leperet, and despite the interest she had sometimes expressed in my presence in the Mahébourg garrison, I wondered if there had not been some change since our voyage to Port Louis, and if it was simply out of affection for me or because he really had need of a rest that Leperet had accepted my invitation.

Thus are destinies gradually fulfilled all around us, slowly and inexorably. Beings who meet after having lived apart for many years come to an understanding and go away together; while others meet, only to invite disaster.

We had taken seats on the veranda. The sound of the receding tide on the reefs reached our ears; a gentle breeze fluttered the lilacs that screened the sea. It was a pleasant afternoon. At any other moment of my existence, doubtless, I should have felt relaxed and happy but, for the past two days, I had missed a certain presence in my life and I knew that more days must pass by before it should be fully restored to me.

It was the period when people from Port Louis and those from Grand Port could not meet without talking about the settlers' trial. Monsieur Boucard asked if there was any hope of the affair being referred to the Assizes. The last reason the government had put forward to explain its dithering was no longer valid, as the assessors to the magistrate for the new year had been nominated more than two months ago.

'What!' exclaimed Souville, 'you still haven't heard? The trial has been set for Monday 10 March.'

'I did not know,' said Monsieur Boucard. 'Doubtless the honour of having you for a passenger made Tronche the coachman lose his head, for the postal bag stayed in Port Louis and we haven't received last week's papers.'

'So you don't know that in London, last November, in the course of a conference at the Colonial Office, d'Epinay was able to tell the Under Secretary of State what he thought of the manner in which the island was governed and of how justice was perceived and executed? The letter from d'Epinay to the Colonial Committee was received four days ago and is dated 22 November. We also talked about Henri Adam, of French origin. Married to a Mauritian, he had taken up residence in the capital in 1817. Before the arrival of the new Governor, he had directed the Volunteer Corps in Port Louis. An expulsion order had been signed against him and he had joined d'Epinay in England to demand the annulment of that order from the Privy Council,' Souville continued.

'You should be thinking seriously about taking Mauritian nationality,' Leperet advised me.

'There is every hope that d'Epinay is finally beginning to be allowed to express his grievances openly,' Souville concluded. 'They had promised him another interview for December so it must have taken place by now.'

'He's a great man,' Madame Boucard *mére* said suddenly; until then, she had not seemed to attach much importance to this political discussion. 'But where I cannot agree with him is when he insists that our customs and our tastes are now English. I am always ready to recognize facts for what they are, but do you think that from one day to the next I could let myself be turned inside out like an old glove?'

Her eyes were flashing. Sometimes, when one suspected her of being angry, one only had to look at the expression in her eyes to be reassured. Nine times out of ten, she was simply enjoying herself prodigiously.

'Mother,' said Monsieur Boucard, 'do you think that, one day, the Mauritians will come to an agreement? Remember the stupid quarrels that opposed the Jacobin partisans to the Bonapartists and those that the royalists had with the Jacobins and the Bonapartists? Monsieur Lepagnez could keep you amused for hours when he recounts the clashes in the veritable theatre of war provided by his hostelry. What is so amusing is that very often the set-to broke out over a trifle. When the antagonists came to blows, they no longer knew why they were fighting – Lepagnez's excellent wine having had a good deal to do with it, naturally. I remember the day when Charles Ghast, who openly touted revolutionary ideas, nearly sent to kingdom come someone who informed him that the Jacobins had worked as cat's paws for Bonaparte. "We worked for the people and not for the individual!" roared Ghast. Whereupon he snatched up an enormous pitcher with which he crowned his luckless opponent.'

The picture this evoked made us smile and then pause. Perhaps just such a pause precedes all things destined, one day or another, to assume great importance.

'I've often wondered . . . I don't know if I'm the only one . . .' Leperet began.

He stopped and coughed slightly.

'Do go on,' urged old Madame Boucard, as implacably as only she knew how.

Leperet cast her an imploring glance.

'You've often wondered,' prompted the old lady, 'how a woman as fine and gracious as Isabelle could have married a man like Charles Ghast, haven't you? Many people in Grand Port have wondered the same thing, you aren't the only one.'

She pulled up her shawl which was sliding from her shoulders and thrust out her chin: 'My own curiosity about the matter has not yet been satisfied,' she added. 'It's no use looking at me like that, Antoine. I say what I think. And you, my dear Jeanne,' she went on, turning towards her daughter-in-law, 'you need not fear that I'm setting your daughters a bad example by interfering in business that does not concern me. Anne and I have already discussed this subject at length, and we weren't just gossiping. Simply curiosity. And there is always a lesson to be learnt from curiosity.'

'I feel sure,' said Monsieur Boucard in his turn, 'that the young woman must have suffered frequently from the contrast between her husband's manners and her own. At the inn, in male company, he conducted himself like a drunken lout before his marriage. Isabelle incontestably had a good influence on him. In public, his behaviour became irreproachable. However, if one is to believe what people say, he made up for it between four walls and they even say that poor Isabelle sometimes had to lock herself in her room until her husband had fallen into a drunken stupor in the drawing-room. It seems that his repentance next morning was always very touching. Like a small boy, he would promise never to start again.'

It was the first time I had heard talk of Charles Ghast. The silence surrounding his name had made me think he was not one whom they received gladly, but I could not be sure. I now began to understand Isabelle's calm: she had learnt it at a good school.

'It was above all on that last evening that I was most struck by his attitude,' said Jeanne Boucard. 'I don't know why, he particularly drew my attention. Perhaps because Isabelle was the prettiest woman in the room and that she had many admirers. It was at Beau Vallon, surely you remember, Antoine? He was leaning against one of the windows. He seemed on tenterhooks. When I saw him moving towards Isabelle and François Kerubec, who had been for a short stroll in the garden between two dances, I thought to myself it would be terrible for his wife if he suddenly took it into his head to turn jealous. But he was all smiles as he went up to them. The next day, we learned that he had died in his sleep.'

'And yet he was of a build to last a hundred years,' said old Madame Boucard, toying with her rings. 'I could just see him with a red bandanna round his head and a pirate's axe in his hand as he boarded some merchant vessel.'

'A burst aneurism or an embolism – I no longer quite remember what the doctor said – gives no warning and spares no one,' said Leperet.

'He didn't even have time to call for help,' said Monsieur Boucard, 'but he fought for his life. Isabelle was wakened by the sound of breaking glass and when she entered his bedroom the carafe on the bedside table had been knocked over. Water was spilt all over the floor.'

'And when Isabelle arrived on the scene . . .?' I asked.

'There was nothing more she could do,' said Antoine Boucard. 'She ran out to call a slave who dashed over to us, another went to wake François. Have you ever noticed how certain things strike you simply because they stand out so clearly in relation to others? In that house where an appalling event had just taken place, I was struck by the festive look of the drawing room. In the four corners of the room, huge red and pink flowers, poinsettias, loomed up out of the vases. They do make impressive bouquets.'

'Isabelle was very courageous,' said Jeanne Boucard. 'I offered her a room here, at least until she had recovered from the shock, but she declined my invitation, saying it was better to get used to her solitary state as soon as possible.'

'Why didn't she come this afternoon?' Madame Boucard *mère* inquired. 'Didn't you invite her, girls?'

'I didn't think of it,' replied Anne briskly.

I seemed to see a smile on Marie-Louise's lips.

A smartly dressed slave, as smartly dressed as Rantanplan, came in bearing glasses, coconut juice and plum brandy.

XIX

The next day at four o'clock Leperet went to call on Isabelle. That morning she had sent him a note. He was over there for quite a while and did not return until the evening, with an anxious look on his face. When all three of us were in the library after dinner, I asked him what had happened.

'What bothers me,' he said, 'is that I cannot understand Madame Ghast's reasons for selling.'

'She clearly explained that she could no longer bear the strain of financial worries,' I replied.

Leperet looked at me with the shadow of a smile.

'Do you really believe that she cannot bear the expense of her estate, and you the purchaser?'

I felt ill at ease as if I had been caught out in a lie.

'My intention is to enlarge the estate,' I said. 'I'm even disposed to offer a price that you may find unreasonable.'

'You put me in a difficult position,' Leperet went on. 'I have to look after the interests of the one as well as of the other. I've arranged an interview with Madame Ghast for Wednesday. We shall visit the estate together – the stores, the slave camp, the big house and all the outbuildings. We shall discuss a price and the next day I shall draw up the sale contract.'

Which is what happened. Isabelle received us, calm and distant, like a stranger. I asked her to excuse my intervention; I had no wish to obtain an expert's assessment, a simple inventory would have sufficed for me. But she broke in: 'Monsieur Leperet has the correct attitude,' she said. 'Let's begin with the offices, the stores and the camp, then we can finish back here in the house. I'll show you the way.'

She put up a white silk parasol and went down the stone stairs. The drive, under its vault of red and pink flowers, came to an end at the national highway. To the right there was the diagonal path. We took the left-hand path.

'Let's look at the stables first,' said Isabelle. 'Three work horses, two saddle horses, a cabriolet, two other carriage horses.'

'But there's no question of carriage horses . . .' I started.

'Everything, Nicolas. I don't want to keep anything. If one day I decided to leave, I'd like to be able to do so within the hour.'

Suddenly anguished, I turned to look at her.

'What curious weariness, Madame Ghast,' said Leperet. 'Kindly allow me, as a friend, to ask you a question. What has got into you?'

She stopped walking and turned back to us. She was smiling. From then on she maintained a lively demeanour and everything seemed to become light and easy once more. 'Nothing Monsieur, I can assure you. But you know how capricious women can be. I wanted to prove that I could run an estate: I have done so. Now I'm tired of it and would like to try something else. What about starting a silkworm farm?'

'A pipe dream,' Leperet replied. 'That's my opinion. Mahé de La Bourdonnais tried it a century ago, at Monplaisir. It was a complete failure. Don't even consider it.'

We had reached the stables. Isabelle was still all smiles. I had the impression that she was congratulating herself on having skilfully diverted Leperet's attention.

I was irritated. 'What's got into them – all this probing of the reasons and actions of others?' I wondered. 'Why not simply be satisfied to accept things as they are now? This is a transaction that concerns only Isabelle and myself, yet we find ourselves having to explain our motives to others and at this rate we'll have to watch out or we'll look like the guilty parties in the case.'

The horses stretched their heads towards us and, recognizing Isabelle, a colt began to neigh. A smell of dry straw rose from the stable litter. A slave went by carrying a bucket of water.

'They're good beasts,' said Isabelle. 'And anyhow you know them, Nicolas.'

At the camp, the slaves stared at us curiously. Perhaps they had already heard talk of our projects. As was the case everywhere, they lived in huts roofed with cane leaves tied in bunches. The half-naked children ran among the huts. Clothes hung on washing-lines and a peaceful atmosphere prevailed. The men were still working in the fields, but the women were already preparing for their return and were busy round wood fires. An old woman, sitting on the beaten earth of a sort of veranda, was peeling manioc. Beside her, on an old sack, a naked baby was waving its arms and legs in the air.

'They never know how to prepare a proper layette,' said Isabelle.

She entered several huts and we could hear her talking in a low voice, asking after the children's health. Replies came from old people in a mournful undertone.

We returned the way we had come. I had never crossed the threshold of Isabelle's house. On our arrival, Leperet and I had waited for her to come out on the veranda. This time, Isabelle lifted a curtain over the entrance to a room.

'Let's get on with it,' she said, 'afterwards we'll have earned some refreshments.'

We entered the drawing-room. In it were grouped pieces of furniture without any kind of style, but the general effect was not displeasing. The same could be said for the dining-room: nothing out of the ordinary. A bachelor's hideaway that a woman had tried to make comfortable by making the best of whatever she had found there, adding little extras that didn't quite go with the rest. A carpet, a mirror, a little writing desk . . .

'And now here is the study. The bedrooms . . .'

'I can assure you, Isabelle, it's not necessary to visit every room. And your apartments . . .'

She looked at me and her face expressed astonishment.

'Why not?' she asked. She cast a glance into the dining room where Leperet was lingering in front of an oil painting. We were alone in the study. She went on in a low voice, that slightly hoarse voice of hers, a strange expression lighting her features: 'I insist, Nicolas. Don't ask why. What a child you are sometimes!'

I followed her into the bedroom. It was all in blue, in every tone of blue. The curtains, the bedspread, the eiderdown, the walls. A broad length of blue tulle was draped around the frame of the mirror. On the dressing table, there were arranged all those objects women cannot do without: scent bottles, toilet water, little bowls, brushes of all shapes and sizes. I drew near, touched a small flask. It was decorated with Isabelle's initials, and I noticed that all the objects laid before me bore the letters I.G. in silver.

'You mustn't laugh at me, Nicolas. I cannot really like a thing, cannot make it truly mine unless it bears my monogram. Obsession, snobbery, call it what you will. I just can't break myself of the habit,' she was adding just as Leperet rejoined us.

We went back on the veranda after having passed through Charles Ghast's bedroom. It was separated from Isabelle's by a small dressing-room. Then we started our discussion. It was certainly the strangest sale Leperet had ever had to handle.

At Isabelle's request, it was decided that she herself would settle all outstanding debts. She explained this to me, saying: 'I've always neglected to keep accounts day by day. I could not show you my account books.'

I assured her it was unnecessary and that I had resolved to start everything on a new footing. It seemed to me that Leperet was not altogether of the same opinion but I did not give him the chance to protest. I said that everything seemed to me to be fair and square and that it was useless to go on with the discussion. I rounded off with a final argument: 'I'm a notary myself,' I said.

'But my dear friend,' he began, 'in certain circumstances . . .'

He stopped, looked from one to the other, smiled and bowed. For a moment, I felt tempted to give his face a good slap. Isabelle had turned her face away towards the drive.

The sale contract was drawn up and signed in the presence of Antoine Boucard and Souville. Neither of them evinced the slightest curiosity. That evening, I gave a dinner for a gathering of several Grand Port estate owners.

On the Friday, at dawn, my two friends took the stagecoach for Port Louis, Leperet having preferred to return to the capital for the opening of the trial of the colonists.

XX

On the afternoon of the same day, I met Isabelle on the diagonal path. The angelus was ringing from the chapel in Mahébourg. The notes reached us quite clearly through the dusk, together with the rumbling of a stagecoach along the national highway.

Perhaps I am lending facts a significance they do not deserve, but I do not judge. The reasons I may have invented, guessed at or accepted are of small importance. A memory which has lain dormant for months can sometimes rise once more out of the shadows and expand in the sun; I stand motionless and mute for a moment, waiting for it to blaze a trail until it possesses its rightful place. I do not exclude the memory of that first encounter after the signature of the sale contract. A wind from somewhere was ruffling the flowering bushes and a heady perfume clung to us from time to time. Seabirds screamed as they passed overhead. Isabelle's demeanour was serious and she was walking slowly, absorbed in her thoughts. We exchanged banal greetings: 'Lovely evening.'

'The heat seems a little less stifling.'

'The wind has turned slightly.'

'We'll have the south-east monsoons before long.'

We were walking side by side and I was thinking I should need to use a lot of tact and show great understanding during the first days. A horse neighed far off and Isabelle suddenly seemed to make up her mind: 'I came here because I knew it would be easy to meet you along the path . . . I must warn you that you should no longer wait for me in the evenings . . . At least for the first two weeks,' she added on seeing my look of surprise. 'We have to consider everything, Nicolas. Think first before you object. I still do not know how the slaves will react to this sale, they may show their displeasure. I want to have a little time to observe them.'

'But Isabelle, look here, that's absurd. People know you will continue to supervise the estate, and they know my slaves are well treated . . .'

I could not insist directly upon the fact that the motive prompting me above all others in our negotiations had been the perservation of our close friendship. I had told her so the first evening, and she could not have forgotten that.

She went to a little rustic bench beside the road and sat down. With lowered eyelids, she started fussing with her lace cuffs and, not knowing why, I suddenly let the memory of our journey in the stagecoach rise to the surface. Leaning back in a corner of the carriage, she was sleeping, and I knew nothing at all about her. Except that I admired her. Now, when she lifted her eyes to mine, the pupils seemed darker than usual.

'Can't you trust me, Nicolas?'

I lowered my head: I knew not what to reply. I had wanted to come closer to her and now felt she was further away than ever. She stood up.

'No, I beg of you – do not accompany me back home.'

She took a few steps, then turned to look back to where I was standing motionless and silent. 'I need a little quiet in order to recover my peace of mind.'

She went on her way. During the days that followed, that mood never altered.

We went on seeing one another every day, in the mornings in the fields, or sometimes in the afternoon on the diagonal path. I could not make out what it was between us and Isabelle did nothing to help me. I sometimes felt that she was hoping or waiting for something, but I did not know what. Then I would tell myself that this attitude was a necessary reaction after a decision that had resulted in what might be considered a sacrifice and that she would require a few weeks to become accustomed to the situation.

The usual routine continued. I had promised Isabelle to help her supervise the work in the fields until the appointment of a new manager. One week after the signing of the sale contract, I selected one of my blacks, Tournesol, and sent him to take charge of Isabelle's slave encampment. Shortly afterwards, as he had the right experience and showed initiative, it was possible to appoint him manager.

Three weeks passed by in this manner. I hardly ever left the estate. The birth of a colt, the pineapple harvest and the ensuing sorting, packing and dispatch by ship to Port Louis occupied several days. Another day was taken up with my concern for a slave. The symptoms he displayed made us suspect poisoning – this was hardly the time to attract the attention of the slave protector at Girofliers. While we awaited the arrival of surgeon Gillet from Mahébourg, Rantanplan disturbed me even further by relating the cases of poisoning he had witnessed amongst the slaves; the result of a quarrel or sometimes just ignorance. When questioned, the sick man's wife told us he had consumed no other food but that which she had prepared for her family. She had carried his mess tin to him in the fields. An hour later, they had carried him into their hut. He was suffering atrociously, could not open his eyes and made great efforts to bring up what he had absorbed; he groaned ceaselessly.

'It reminds me of the case of Entêté's daughter at Ghast's,' Rantanplan told me in a low voice. 'It was pitiful to see the poor child's struggles. As soon as she fell sick, Madame Ghast sent over to us for help. She was all alone on the estate. Monsieur Charles had left the night before for Port Louis. Monsieur François asked me to accompany him because I know some simple remedies. The girl was making the same huge efforts to vomit as you see here and kept writhing on her palliasse. Monsieur François rode into Mahébourg to try to find the surgeon and bring him back with him. But when he got back here, it was all over.'

'But what had she eaten?' I asked, less out of curiosity than to quieten my anxiety.

'Later, we tried to put two and two together, and we discovered that her mother was busy sweeping Madame Ghast's drive when the child rolled on the ground in a sort of convulsive fit. It was thought she had plucked or picked up one of the red flowers in the drive and chewed at it. The surgeon said it was a fatal poison. Since then, Madame Ghast has forbidden children to enter her courtyard. I also witnessed the sufferings of Canapé when his brother mixed crushed *bambara* with his rice . . .'

He was interrupted by the rumbling of a carriage and I went to meet the surgeon. We were all greatly relieved when the surgeon diagnosed sunstroke and administered a sedative draft. But the slave, and all of us, had had a narrow escape.

And so the days passed by.

XXI

At Port Louis, the Grand Port trial went on day after day at the Assizes. We had no hint of what the outcome might be. We were awaiting the verdict, on some days lapsing into a kind of numb despair, then taking heart once more. Monsieur Boucard had given up all idea of going to Port Louis: 'If they are sentenced, I shall lose control!'

The news-sheets were even more violent. In the last week of March they reported that the verdict would be given on the 29th. They pointed out that the trial had taken eighteen hearings.

On the morning of the 29th, a Saturday, life was flowing along, apparently as calmly as ever, on all the estates. The slaves were called out at dawn and work was distributed among the various groups. At midday, we began to hand out the rations as usual. But in the afternoon, conveyances clattered by along the roads and horsemen passed at a gallop. Whenever two riders met, one of them would make a half turn to meet the other and then would continue on his way. It seemed as if all were living in hope of a miracle.

As soon as I had finished my inspection of the storehouses, I hurried back to the house. I prepared myself and went to see Monsieur Boucard. I found him pacing up and down on his terrace. 'It's ridiculous,' he shouted as soon as he saw me, 'I just can't settle down to do anything.'

'You're not the only one,' I answered.

'They're trying to calm their impatience by possibly riding off to get news,' he went on, 'But we can't know anything before tomorrow evening. We must be reasonable. Would you like to take a turn down on the beach with me?' he asked, picking up his walking stick.

We tried to evaluate the true effect of the witnesses' depositions and thus to deduce what the consequences would be, but we came up against innumerable difficulties. One of Monsieur de Robillard's slaves had testified against his master by relating a garbled version of a conversation he had overheard when serving at table. For his part, the Governor had criticized the prisoners for the terms they had used in addressing themselves to him. His Excellency also disapproved of the publicity given by the newspapers to letters exchanged between him and the accused. All in all, we were unable to curb our disquiet.

The day was coming to an end. The fishing boats were returning to the shore. We heard voices and saw Marie-Louise, Anne and Isabelle coming down the avenue. They were coming towards us and I got the impression all at once that people and nature were basking in total serenity. It seemed that Isabelle had overcome her nervous depression. Her face had regained its calm and again, without knowing why, I began to think of the stay we had made at Port Louis. Then, everything had seemed to be so easy for me. Five months had gone by, but the time had not seemed long.

Isabelle and her companions sat on the grassy slope beside us. I looked at Isabelle. There was a kind of radiance in her face, in her eyes. The nightmare of the past weeks was dissipating. She was that smiling, frail woman, more or less abandoned to her fate, who appealed to me so much; she whose hand I hoped to take one day to conduct her across the threshold of Girofliers.

I suddenly realized they were talking about the marriage of one of Anne's schoolfriends. Anne had agreed to be a bridesmaid.

'Do you realize what that means?' said Monsieur Boucard. 'Fifty metres of Indian muslin, the hat, the gloves, the buskins, hours simpering in front of the mirror, dressmaker and heaven knows what else!'

Marie-Louise spoke of the next visit by Madame Rose, the fashion arbiter. For a few minutes the conversation continued on this theme, then Anne turned to me.

'I forgot to mention it to you, Nicolas – grandmamma has expressed the desire to speak to you as soon as possible. If you have no objection, I'll take you to her now.'

I begged my companions to excuse me and followed Anne. We kept in step as we walked. I liked her youthful gaiety and felt full of affection for her. Yet whenever we were alone together I always felt a little ill at ease. In my eyes, she was only a child, but I could not treat her as one. I tried teasing her: 'Friends of your age are getting married, Anne,' I told her. 'Soon it will be your turn. Perhaps you'll move far away, to an unknown house.'

'I don't know if I shall marry,' she replied earnestly. 'It's a very serious decision to make. Just think – it's for life!'

Her gravity amused me.

'When one's mind is filled with thoughts of love, one no longer considers whether the question is serious or not. One just enjoys life – giving all one's being to happiness.'

She turned to me abruptly.

'What do *you* know about it?' she demanded.

'Anne, soon I shall be thirty, so it seems to me I may speak a little from experience of the world,' I replied, trying to keep the conversation on a playful level.

'Do you really think that under any circumstances one could love someone whom . . . whom one despised? Someone living – living what one might call a lie?'

I could not mask my astonishment.

'Can it be that you love someone like that?'

I hesitated over my choice of words; I was trying to understand; I was telling myself that we often live with people without really knowing them. But then Anne made one of those impatient gestures I was beginning to be wary of: her right arm lifted then dropped.

'You are silly, Nicolas! What have I got to do with it? I'm trying to put my thoughts in order. Answer my question.'

'Anne, what can I say? It seems to me such things do happen. There are examples in history; we are far from being models of virtue.'

I was stumbling over each phrase and wondered what she was getting at, what she was really thinking.

She stopped and looked at me. I sensed she was overcome by emotion and I could have sworn she was on the brink of tears.

'So it means,' she said, 'that life is ugly and dirty, that nothing can ever be beautiful again, and that amorous impulse . . .'

She went no further in the expression of her thoughts, doubtless because she knew her voice was betraying her agitation and distress. I murmured something vague: 'Come now, you must not . . .'

'That's enough,' she said. 'Don't say another word.'

I felt as abashed as a child who has just been scolded. We were approaching the Boucard house, but we stopped a little way from the entrance steps and Anne said to me in her normal voice: 'So you've enlarged your estate now!'

'Yes,' I answered, feeling relieved, and on much safer ground with this subject. 'Ever since I arrived here, I've been wanting to buy land and start to build something new on my own.'

'I have to ask you something else, Nicolas. When one has a bank account, can one have financial worries?'

'Naturally, that all depends upon what transactions one undertakes. If you bear the upkeep of a property, for example, it means great expense. The money one possesses may not always be enough to cover all obligations.

I gave these explanations in all seriousness. I felt within me something that was at one and the same time a mixture of curiosity and pity.

'When you put money in the bank, Nicolas, they send you a letter telling you: "I have the honour to inform you that your account has reached the amount of . . ."?'

I smiled and told myself I had been wrong to see this girl in a tragic light. She was an inquisitive, nervous child and her imagination sometimes carried her away – further perhaps than she desired.

'Certainly,' I replied, 'particularly if you have taken the trouble to send a letter to the bank manager along the lines: "Sir, I should be grateful if you would acquaint me with . . ."'

I had deliberately employed a rather inflated mode of address to amuse her and create a diversion, but she remained poker-faced.

'And when you have fifty thousand piastres in the bank, Nicolas, can you . . . can you still have money troubles?'

I started to laugh.

'It's possible, but when you possess fifty thousand piastres you can always make ends meet.'

Madame Boucard *mère* leaned out of the drawing-room window and called to us: 'What are you children plotting?'

'Here we are, grandmamma!' cried Anne. And through clenched teeth: 'Bitch!'

I thought I had not heard right, 'What was that you said, Anne?'

We were mounting the stone staircase, 'I said: 'Bitch'!'

'Anne!'

She turned towards me and her eyes were flashing in a kind of cold rage: 'So what? Another of the words one must not use, I suppose?'

She went before me as far as the drawing-room door, but did not cross the threshold. 'I'm leaving you Nicolas, grandmamma,' she said in a smooth voice.

She left me speechless and I had to muster all my presence of mind to offer my greetings to the old dame.

'I was beginning to miss you,' Madame Boucard said, 'so I asked the young girls to let you know. It seems a long time since we had the opportunity to have a quiet chat together.'

She invited me to draw up a chair. Her sharp eyes never left my face. She had pushed aside the little table on which stood the wooden block, bristling with pins, for her pillow lace. The spindles were arranged on either side of the block and attached to the lace by threads that had to be criss-crossed in a certain order to obtain designs of an incomparable delicacy and lightness.

'There really have been some changes, haven't there, since last we met?' went on Madame Boucard.

I smiled. 'And have you summoned me to congratulate or to accuse?'

'It is not for me either to accuse or to congratulate you,' she said.

'So far no one has censured me for buying new land, but I seem to detect a certain reticence in the words employed by all those who mention it to me. You'd never believe, Madame Boucard,' I went on, 'how much that embarrasses and irritates me, if I may be so frank with you.'

'If we could always be as frank,' commented the old lady, turning the rings on her fingers, 'perhaps we could be of greater service to others. But we cannot, we dare not, despite all our affection for them. And then we tell ourselves that, after all, everything ends satisfactorily, that we judged things wrongly, or rather that our judgement was distorted by circumstance . . .'

She raised her head: 'Does all this nonsense I'm spouting surprise you, Nicolas?'

'No,' I replied, 'I'm just wondering. I am still not accustomed to seeing my slightest gestures acquiring such great importance. Are people really so interested in my welfare, or is it simply idle curiosity?'

'In the colonies, one cannot stop people prying and commenting on one's private life. Besides, it's not the first time . . .'

She did not finish her sentence and started to roll the fringes of her shawl round her fingers.

'Look, Nicolas,' she went on, 'it's better that you should be warned. Antoine and his wife are not of my opinion and think we should not bore you with these idle rumours. But I'm an old woman, I reason differently, perhaps I even ramble on too much but I am of the opinion that you should be made aware of what's going on. People long ago started gossiping about your close friendship with Isabelle, and during the past weeks their comments have taken on a spiteful note. You're still not familiar with our way of life here . . .'

I began to feel anger mounting in me and I interrupted Madame Boucard without a word of apology: 'And what are they saying?'

'What do you expect people to say – can't you guess? The fact that you've bought the estate and that she continues to occupy the house and oversee the work has given people fresh food for speculation.'

'I must admit that I expected it. But I thought things would settle down quickly.'

'We do whatever is in our power, but, of course, in our presence, such allusions are not ill-natured. A touch of irony at most. We can't start tilting at windmills. And then, it seems to me that it's up to you to put an end to this situation.'

Night was falling and shadows were slowly permeating the room. Beside me, on a low table, a rose scattered its petals. I do not know how the question came to my lips: 'What do you advise me to do?'

The old dame turned her face towards me and asked: 'You really want to know what I think? Whatever it is?'

'Yes,' I replied tonelessly.

'May God forgive me, but I don't like that woman. I have never liked that woman.' There was a pause. There was a tap at the door and a slave entered bringing in a lamp.

'Antoine tells me that you're filling in the marshes. It's an excellent idea. No one had thought of doing that until now.'

'It's quite possible I shall install a steam-driven sugar refinery.'

We had regained our self-possession.

'It's getting late,' I said.

'I'll set you at liberty again. I'll call Anne . . .'

She opened a door and cried 'Anne' in a rousing voice, but the young girl did not answer.

'She's probably gone back down to the beach. Please do not bother.'

I wished her good-night.

'May the Lord watch over you, Nicolas,' she replied.

I rejoined the group still lingering on the shore. Anne was not among them. A half moon was rising above the casuarinas, shedding a cold radiance. Something, a piece of mother-of-pearl or sea-smoothed glass, was shining in the sand.

'I was counting on you to escort me home, Nicolas,' said Isabelle.

We took leave of the others.

'Let's all meet again tomorrow,' Antoine Boucard shouted after us.

I knew he was thinking of the trial. Tomorrow by this time we should know the outcome. At Port Louis, people already knew whether to rejoice or feel dismay. 'Whatever the result of the trial,' I told Isabelle, 'it would seem that a new life is about to begin.'

We had reached the avenue leading up to Girofliers and walking was no longer so difficult. In the dry sand, we had sunk in at each step. Before entering the avenue we turned to look back at the ocean.

'A new life!' Perhaps we expect too much of life, Nicolas. If we consider it with detachment, perhaps we'll reach the conclusion that it's already wonderful enough just to exist and to possess those things that no one can take away from us – the sun, our walks by the sea, a rest under a tree . . .'

'What a delight it is to see you like this again, Isabelle!'

'Again?'

I detected a touch of impatience in her voice.

'It's not a reproach, I'm just stating a fact.'

'Nicolas, women get nervous and irritable at times, you mustn't hold it against us. Sometimes they don't think enough. They follow their instincts, which is not always advisable. Fortunately everything gets settled in the end.'

A flame suddenly burned brightly on the shore of the Ile aux Fouquets, then a second, a third and a fourth.

'The bush telegraph,' said Isabelle. 'A turtle has been caught. The people on the Ile aux Fouquets are asking for a boat big enough to transport it.'

'You'll never stop surprising me, Isabelle! You, a foreigner, have come to understand all these things, when the majority of people who have settled here must be ignorant of them. How many, in Mahébourg this evening, would have understood the message sent out by the blacks on the Ile aux Fouquets?'

'I never felt bored here because I always wanted to understand everything.'

We turned back to go home.

'Do you often bathe in the sea, Nicolas?' she asked.

'Sometimes,' I replied.

'There's a marvellous spot near here. In the past, from time to time, I used to enjoy bathing there after dinner; I had only just arrived. On nights of the full moon I would escape from the house to the beach. All that now seems so far away,' she added regretfully.

I suddenly felt a strange force mounting within me. It was like one of those great groundswells that overturn everything in their course.

'And you were alone?'

She cast me a look in which I seemed to read both curiosity and a kind of satisfaction. 'Of course, what do you think . . .?'

'I think it strange that a young woman of twenty should go down to the beach alone at night in a foreign land.'

'What is there to be afraid of?'

'Everything.'

'And don't I go out alone at night now?'

'It's not the same thing!'

She started to laugh and repeated my last words: 'It's not the same thing!'

She stopped and turned back again to look at the ocean. The expression on her face gradually changed and became pensive; her eyelids fluttered nervously.

'Perhaps it's not the same thing, because my knight in shining armour Nicolas is here now . . .'

'And what difference does that make?'

'It makes no difference. After ten years . . .'

She did not finish her sentence. If only she had finished it . . . But these reticences aroused in me that obscure jealousy I had been trying in vain to resist. I sensed she was back in those times that were not mine to share with her. Days in which she had thought, walked and loved also. I looked at her and felt at one and the same time the impulse to crush her in my arms and beat her. Beat her until she had forgotten everything belonging to her former life, everything she had known before that moment when I had found her in the corridor at Port Louis.

I watched her fluttering her eyelids and biting the corner of her lips. I caught her by the arms.

'What's got into you?' I asked harshly.

She seemed to come back from far away, but it was I who took my face in my hands. We went on our way in silence. What could I have said that she did not already know? When we reached the diagonal path, she spoke calmly and gently: 'Don't bother coming any further. It's as clear as day. I'll be all right going home alone.'

And as I was about to protest, she laid a finger on her lips.

XXII

The next morning, as he brought in my breakfast tray, Rantanplan asked me to take a look at the garden. I propped myself up on my pillows. Through the window as far as the eye could see a sheet of pink extended between the clove trees. Thousands of little lilies had flowered during the night and were crowded motionless beneath the foliage.

'I had heard about this, but it's the first time I've seen it. Is it a good omen, Rantanplan?'

He started to laugh, his whole face gently wrinkling. 'It's usually the sign of rain and storms,' he said.

'But the sky's bright blue.'

'You should take a look at the sky over the Mont du Lion.'

As I was going to Mass, I noted that the slopes on either side of the road were in bloom and all the gardens in Mahébourg had their own rosy mantle. Behind the mountain, crouching on the horizon, a big black cloud was gathering.

At Mass I found Isabelle calm and distant. She did not turn her head to look at me when I arrived. When we came out, she mingled with the Boucard clan and we exchanged a few words. The girls invited her home for a mid-morning coffee, but she refused. She said she had letters to write and many other things to attend to, and she had promised herself she would devote her afternoon to these.

Conversation was animated on the little square. The newspapers and letters that had arrived the previous evening were all subjects of comment. Monsieur Boucard and I decided we should get in touch as soon as either one of us had news from Port Louis.

I went home. The heat of the sun was oppressive and I regretted having sent back the carriage. An odour of dried straw hung on the air. The great silence of Sunday brought clearly to my ears the lowing cattle in the pasture. A dog ran along the road, trampling on the pink lilies, then swerved off into a field, his ears pricked up. The road, dusty and cracked, stretched away between the sugar-canes. A little cart pulled by a donkey passed by, driven by a white-haired negress. The donkey had a big red bow tied to his neck and was trotting along in a cloud of dust.

I lingered in the garden where new fruit-tree stocks had just been planted. In the ornamental pool, paradise fish were swimming among the weeds.

Luncheon, a little reading and a siesta occupied the rest of the afternoon. I was getting ready, despite the threatening black clouds, to go and try to get some news when Monsieur Boucard arrived. A courier from Port Louis had just reached Mahébourg announcing the acquittal of the five settlers.

'I've come to find you,' said Monsieur Boucard, 'because we are preparing a reception for them this afternoon at Lepagnez's. We think they'll be here around five o'clock. They're coming in a private carriage. After stopping off at their homes they'll join us all at Lepagnez's place.

Lepagnez's inn had probably never echoed with so much noise and talk. We crowded round our neighbours and everyone made a point of demonstrating his sympathy for them. Questions and answers flew back and forth. Nevertheless one sensed that our friends would prefer to forget the past months.

Lepagnez brought out his best vintages. Under the arbour, songs and laughter came from a group of young people. Two or three members of the garrison, attracted by the noise coming from the inn, were served glasses of wine then politely departed. Just as we were exchanging vows of eternal friendship, someone proposed dining at the inn. Some people asked to be excused and followed Monsieur Boucard and his companion. The latter were anxious to get back to their families and no one insisted on their staying.

There were about fifteen of us left round a groaning board on which Lepagnez soon set an enormous ham omelette. We had forgotten the black clouds massing above Mahébourg and suddenly the rain started: big drops that splashed on the tiles and crashed against the windows. Then it fell harder and denser, awakening ripe old smells of drenched earth and grass. A flash of lightning, followed by others, lit the darkness, and, sitting facing the window, I saw, plucked out of the night but veiled in mists, a corner of the bay.

A crash of thunder often drowned the noise of voices. Sometimes a more trenchant clap cut short a boastful laugh. But the clamour rumbled away into the distance and gradually grew fainter. The gurgle of rain in the gutters filled rare moments of silence.

The omelette was followed by three plump chickens roasted on a spit accompanied by a salad of cress from the garden. When the meal was over, we had to wait for another hour before being able to set off home. Two young men from Beau Vallon offered to take me back in their carriage. As soon as it began to clear up, the horses were led out of the stables and put into harness. Mellowed by mazers of wine, we exchanged emotional adieux. 'A memorable evening!' cried Lepagnez, standing in his doorway to wave us godspeed.

We hardly said a word during the drive, as if we had exhausted our reserves of gaiety and conviviality. Half-way home, the head of one of my companions dropped on my shoulder and I allowed it to remain there until we got to Girofliers. The night air had the reverse effect on me for I felt refreshed and regretted not being able to return home on foot. The horses were ambling along. The rain was still falling fitfully in brief showers and the carriage lamps lit the puddles of water on the road. The conveyance stopped in front of the avenue.

In the house only the ground floor was lit up. Rantanplan, knowing I would be returning later after the events of the afternoon, had made the rounds of the upstairs lamps. But he was not lacking in thoughtfulness; on the dining table, a cold collation had been laid out for me.

I took off my jerkin, pulled off my muddy boots, washed my face and hands. At slippered ease, I went to the library and lay down on the big corner couch. The rain had stopped. A strange sense of peace flowed over me. Within me and all around me, I felt a sort of renewal taking strength from the coolness, the silence, the first stars.

Upstairs, a shutter banged against the wall and the sound echoed through the house. I looked for the book I had chosen from the library shelves, but I did not open it. The curtains' fitful movement imitated the flight of the frigate bird, gliding downwards on outstretched wings; I almost seemed to see a blue sky and a huge bird. For a second time the wooden shutter clacked noisily upstairs and I thought I should have to go and fix it before going to bed. Yet I lingered over this excess of delight. I snuggled deeper into the cushions. It's impossible to say whether I lay there ten minutes or sixty. Suddenly a milky luminosity bathed the terrace and I thought of the clouds drifting apart and releasing the light of the moon. In the trees, a few birds, surprised, began to chatter, then fell silent one by one.

Upstairs, the shutter banged a third time, and with such violence the crystal and opaline baskets in the drawing room vibrated a long time in the glass cabinet. I stood up, took a lighted candle and moved towards the small stairwell behind the library. I went up, the candle flame fluttering slightly as I gazed at my shadow dancing on the wall. On the landing, I checked the shutters and the windows. The hooks were in place and I went through the other rooms. I leaned out of François' window for a few moments, wondering at the calm of the fields. Not a leaf was stirring; the trees soared proudly aloft. The stars were scintillating as if they had been freshly washed by the rain.

Nor did I find anything out of the ordinary in the bedchamber of François II. I crossed the landing again and opened the door of the rose silk bedchamber. But I stopped short on the threshold. On an armchair, near the window, there was a grey dress covered with rosebuds. I shoved open the door and lit up the room. Other feminine garments had been thrown on other chairs. I walked right in and stopped at the foot of the canopied four-poster. Lying there, the rose satin counterpane drawn up to her neck, her long, unbound hair spread out on the pillow, Isabelle was looking at me.

She sat up, leaning on an elbow. 'I was caught by the rainstorm . . .'

It was the voice of a child caught redhanded in some forbidden game. I did not answer. What did it matter? I was wondering when the counterpane would stop sliding down: I could see only a rounded shoulder gradually being bared. I gazed at it and it seemed to me as if I were tasting it like a fruit. Nothing else existed but that round and gleaming shoulder, that dark hair, that face and also that ardour and that violence I felt mounting in me. Nothing else had any meaning and I accepted the fact that this woman with the anxious eyes was taking control of my mind, my happiness and my pain, my laughter and my tears, my breath . . . I went and placed the candlestick on the beside table.

XXIII

Well before daybreak, I went down to my bedroom. From my wardrobe, I chose a pair of navy blue trousers and a white silk shirt. All was sleeping still. Outside, the moon having completed its course, the darkness was profound. Another half-hour, one hour, and the demesne would awaken from its silence.

Upstairs, the clothes were still not dry.

'I could wear a disguise . . .' Isabelle had said.

I went back upstairs and laid out the trousers and shirt in the bathroom. When Isabelle reappeared dressed as a young man, she still had not put up her hair. I went up to her, pulled back her head as my fingers stroked that dark mass.

I looked into her eyes; her face was relaxed and happy.

I gazed at her and a phrase came back to mind: 'May God forgive me, I don't like that woman, I have never liked that woman.' My fingers slid gently downwards . . .

We parted on the terrace. She refused to let me go with her. 'If by chance I should meet someone, it would be better for me to be alone.'

I allowed the white splash of the shirt to disappear into the night, then I went back upstairs. Isabelle had made the bed, spread the counterpane. She had taken with her her light underwear, but her heavy dress was still on the armchair and I had to take it up to the attics. First I tried to put everything in order in the bathroom. Isabelle's soaking shoes had left marks on the parquet. When the room had been restored to its usual state, I threw the grey dress over my arm and closed the door.

XIV

Up in the attics, where I had gone for the first time, I hung the dress from a coat-peg to let it dry. I knew that the servants rarely went up there except to store unwanted furniture or objects that were not in regular use. By the light of a candle, I recognized my travel bags that had been deposited next to some trunks with brass studs. I was in a hurry. I ran down the little staircase from the attics as the cocks were beginning to crow. From my bedroom, I heard a stable door slam and the feed-buckets clunking. I thought of the shutter I hadn't closed but shrugged it off. I lay down between the sheets and fell sound asleep.

When I opened my eyes the clock stood at nine. On a table beside my bed, the coffee was cold. Rantanplan hadn't dared wake me and I hadn't heard the bell for starting work.

I hurriedly got ready. Upstairs, the servants were waxing the parquet. Life went on as usual all round me and I wondered if it was possible for everything to be just as always – the men in the fields, the baker at his oven in the basement, the oxen harnessed to the carts and the waggoners keeping in step with the slow but steady pace of their teams.

I paused a moment at the window. The pink lilies had vanished, drowned in last night's rain and mud, but the clove trees were lifting up their bunches of cloves to the morning sun.

I had Taglioni saddled. I felt the need to ride off alone down some broad, endless road. The slaves were stripping the sugar-canes on the slopes of Mont Créole. The rain had lent a fresh lustre to the leaves and grass, and steam was rising from the earth. On my way back, I stopped to check the filling-in of the ponds. Last night's rain had stopped the work. In another day or two, the team of labourers, under Vigilant's direction, would be starting work again. At the foot of Mont Créole, I tried to imagine what the landscape would look like once the drainage of the land was completed. The fields would stretch right down to the ocean in a vast flat slope, with only the little clump of trees I intended to leave around the place where François' body had been found. Another eight to ten months and the refinery's smoke-stack would be rising somewhere down there. That morning no project could seem too ambitious for me. I lost myself in endless daydreams. Some of us retain, from our caveman ancestors, a taste for danger and an urge to conquer and dominate; however, it may so happen that life takes us far beyond what we had hoped for. Last night, I had lived out a dream far more wonderful than anything I had ever expected. I felt powerful and triumphant.

The mare was trotting along and a wind from the sea whipped my face. I started to sing at the top of my voice; the slaves I passed stared after me. When I arrived home, Ballet de Rosine was on the terrace, a broad smile on her face. 'It is like in Monsieur François' day,' she said.

I thought of what Rantanplan had told me on my first day there. If he had not been inspecting some work in the fields, no doubt he too would have come to meet me, the same phrase on his lips.

After luncheon, as soon as everything had fallen silent in the basement, I went up into the attics. The sun was shining through the skylights. The dress was still hanging from its coat-peg. I touched it. It felt dry and sent out a delicate floral scent. I went to a dormer window and pressed my forehead to the glass; that dress and that perfume now invading all my senses . . . To what even greater excesses might not my imagination deliver me? I knew that we should not allow ourselves to let the imagination go in such a facile manner. 'It seems to me that it's up to you to put an end to this situation,' Madame Boucard had said. The moment had arrived.

I turned round. Nothing takes you out of yourself so completely as the mysterious atmosphere of an attic. For a whole century, the one at Girofliers had been gradually filled up with the most heteroclite assortment of objects. Wing chairs and trunks, old beds with mattresses of woven bast, tables with cracked marble tops; all the bric-à-brac of haphazard accumulation over the years was piled up under the rooftiles of Girofliers.

I paused in front of an old cradle, its wood sculpted into rosettes and tiny columns. Right next to it, as if to serve as a seat for mother or nurse, they had set a large chest ornamented with the same sculptures. I felt as if the years had rolled away and that I was once more a boy on holiday. In a farm kitchen, next to the window, there had been a cradle similar to the one I now beheld. And beside it there was the very same chest, a marriage chest, the sort in which a young Breton bride in olden times would transport her trousseau. Both cradle and marriage chest had belonged to Catherine Couessin. They were covered with a fine layer of dust. I thought of the hand that had polished these objects more than a century ago. I thought also of the young woman who had embarked one morning at Nantes or at Lorient, of the man accompanying her who had promised her love and security and who, ever faithful, had come back home to bring her here, to this concession he had acquired, for better or for worse. Down in the hold lay the cradle and the marriage chest. It was easy to imagine that these things had been chosen with love. Doubtless their purpose was to bring to mind the traditions of the homeland in a foreign country. I had learnt from the family record that the cradle had not been used until nine years later and under this very roof. Forty-four years later, another woman's hands had prepared it under the watchful gaze of the grandmother-to-be. Then the baby had grown up, and once again the cradle had been taken up into the attic.

The galloping of a horse broke into my reverie. Rantanplan was coming back from the fields. He would be coming to find me to arrange as usual the work programme for the following day. I took the dress, folded it clumsily and stuffed it into the marriage chest. There were other clothes in there, but I had neither the time nor the curiosity to examine them more closely.

When Rantanplan tapped at the library door, I was seated in my accustomed place at the writing desk, opening the account book. What hypocrisy there is in what we call the nobility of toil! I know now that work cannot bring fulfilment to a life unless we have already lost that life. Otherwise it is just a necessity or an accessory, a means of commanding the esteem of others or of oneself, a wager. It becomes a sacred calling only if we have entirely given up all hope of anything else.

The rest of the day dragged on. Tea was served. I felt more and more restless as the hours passed by. I visited the stables. The horses were standing with their heads outside their boxes and a young slave – it was Cupidon, son of Rantanplan – was currying Taglioni. The sun was descending towards the horizon, its oblique rays entering the fanlights, gilding the straw of the litter, and in that golden stream of light one could see the dust rising from the animal's coat. Another slave came in and shook out some hay and freshly cut grass. The horses were pawing the ground in their impatience, their hooves ringing on the cobbles. The stable lad ran his hand over the mane, stroking it a moment while he poured each ration of grain into the feeding trough and also piled up in it handfuls of grass. Jaws began to crunch the feed with a calm, regular rhythm. Tails whipped at flanks. Heads dipped and rose. I got the impression of watching some kind of ritual and this ritual had the curious power of appeasing me. I left the stables and walked towards the avenue. Once again, I thought I only had to wait.

To wait for the moment when I should find myself once more in the presence of Isabelle.

XXV

That night, she did not come. In my heart of hearts, I knew she would not do so and yet I had not been able to give up expecting her. After the first hours had gone by, I had to exert a great effort of will not to go running to her. I could envision her blue bedroom. I could see her as she had appeared to me the night before. I remembered the silken softness of her skin and I felt my hands shaking. I sat on the rail of the terrace balustrade. So profound a peace reigned over the fields that I could hear the murmuring of the stream gliding down to the ocean, behind the outhouses. The great avenue stretched before my eyes, tranquil and deserted. The palms bowed their heads at the least breath of wind and glittered under the moon.

Like a lovesick boy, I went over the events of the day before one by one, from the morning onwards, compelling myself to remember every detail, always putting off the moment when I would plunge myself into what was both my ecstasy and the exaltation of my pride. I went back into the house and began the round of the lamps. But I stopped on the threshold of Catherine Couessin's bedchamber. The memories I had been repressing all day long and all evening flooded back. As on the night before, I placed the lighted candle in its silver candlestick on the bedside table. As on the night before, I lifted the counterpane and turned it back. I cast myself upon the vast bed, my face buried in its silken folds, my fingers searching for the warm and supple mass of unbound tresses and their perfume of flowers.

Shortly after the call to work next morning, while I was taking breakfast in the library, Rantanplan entered and stood by the door, motionless, his eyes fixed upon me. It was the attitude he adopted whenever he had something to tell me but did not venture to disturb me; he was waiting for me to ask the usual question; I finished pouring my cup of tea and set down the teapot:

'Did you wish to speak to me, Rantanplan?'

'Yes, master, but it's difficult for me.'

'Just let me know what it is.'

He seemed to be searching for suitable words, then decided to speak at last: 'Tournesol is here, in the kitchen.'

The presence of Isabelle's manager surprised me. It was agreed that Isabelle would continue to give the orders and Tournesol knew that. I wondered if it was the start of some kind of mutiny.

'What does he want?'

I think my voice must have been harsh and overpowering. Rantanplan took a few steps towards me. He slipped his hands between his broad leather belt and his shirt, which in him was a sign of great embarrassment.

'He asked me to explain to you . . . You must understand, master. Nothing like that has been done here for years, and Tournesol is just a young lad, he's not accustomed to it. He thinks you might possibly intervene . . .'

'I do not understand, Rantanplan. Intervene? How?'

He came a little nearer and this time spoke very quickly: 'Tournesol was given the command to give thirty lashes of the whip to Introuvable.'

I tried to hide my feelings.

'Introuvable must have done something very bad?'

Rantanplan turned his eyes away from me. 'Possibly, master. He left his work yesterday morning and stayed in camp.'

'Was he sick?'

'No, it's his wife, she's had a baby boy. When they came to tell him the news, he left the field and went back to the camp. His absence was noticed and he was called back. He refused the order to return.'

'Has he many children?'

'This is their first, master.'

'Did Tournesol go back to the fields?' I asked.

'Yes, it was when he got back there, at ten, that he . . .'

'Very well,' I broke in, 'tell him to return to work.'

'Is that all, master?'

'That's all.'

He seemed to be hesitating, probably not satisfied with my curt reply. I chose one of the last mangoes of the season from the fruitbowl. Rantanplan understood that our interview was over.

I could not allow a black to be flogged on my estate. Perhaps for the first time since I had purchased Isabelle's property, I realized the extent of my new responsibilities. Until then, I had contented myself with a few rounds of the plantations in the company of Isabelle. We would walk along the roads and along the footpaths, she leading me, I seeing only the graceful curve of her hips, the movements of her slightly lifted skirt on the flat walking shoes tied at the ankles by criss-crossed ribbons. Sometimes, with her white parasol tipped back on her shoulder, she would turn back to me and I would see the brilliance of her smile, the sparkle of her eyes between the lids. How could I have paid any attention to other things? The conversation I had just had with Rantanplan had brought me brutally back to reality.

By enlarging Girofliers, by purchasing new slaves, it was my duty to treat them like Kerubec ones, following principles laid down by my cousin. During the difficult periods of the last few months, I could only derive satisfaction from this stance. I had neither the right nor the desire to depart from established custom. Yet I felt a repugnance in having to talk about these matters with Isabelle. European by birth, as she was, albeit brought up in a totally different atmosphere, it seemed to me that we should have had the same reactions and the same way of looking at things, and it had not been without a certain unease that I had noted how the human herd included in the list of goods I had inherited was inscribed between the beasts and the waggons. What seemed normal to the majority of Mauritians, accustomed since childhood to treat their blacks as beasts of burden, offended my sense of equality. And as for using the whip to punish them, it was an idea I could not accept.

A quarter of an hour later, I was walking Taglioni along the diagonal path. I was feeling disappointed, tense. This was not how I had envisaged my first meeting with Isabelle after we . . . Judging by the height of the sun, I realized that it was still very early, for the days are relatively long at that time of the year. It was about seven o'clock. We were now at the beginning of April. The earth was humid and there were still drops of dew on the sugar-cane leaves. I watched them sparkling and wondered what I should say to Isabelle in order to persuade her to call off Introuvable's punishment. Until today, she had seemed to be all goodness and kindness. I knew she was benevolent and that she could feel deep concern for others, even if that concern caused her great inconvenience. She had not hesitated to spend three days in an uncomfortable country inn in order to take care of Madame Cochrane. It was the first time that altriusm had been demonstrated in my presence. I could remember having been both moved and exasperated by it at the time.

When I reached Isabelle's house, a servant came to meet me and told me her mistress was out in the fields, somewhere around the dry ravine, she thought, where they were planting maize. I started off again in that direction. I found Isabelle standing on some raised ground overlooking the field. Her figure stood out against the clear sky. She was looking in my direction and probably had heard Tagilioni's hoofbeats. Eyes half-closed, she watched me approaching through those lids that sloped slightly upwards to the temples. I dismounted. I was forgetting why I had come to meet her until the moment when, having shaken the hand she held out to me, I turned back to the ploughed field to try to conquer the strange weakness I suddenly felt sweeping over me. And all at once I saw Tournesol. His eyes were upon us and an expectant look softened his features. It was all I needed to bring me back to the realization of what my people expected of me.

'I have to speak to you, Isabelle,' I said.

She smiled, her face rosy beneath the parasol.

'I'm all yours . . .'

'Perhaps we should move away a bit, I wouldn't want the slaves to hear.'

'Oh . . . what little they would gather of . . .'

But she went down the steps cut out of the earth. On the footpath, I took Taglioni by the bridle. We were moving slowly in the direction of Mont Créole. The sun was gilding the crests of the Grand Port chain, but on the mountain slopes mist was lingering here and there. Sometimes swooping down as if it had emerged from a dark cave, a long-tailed bird of prey would launch itself from a peak. We watched it hovering before gliding down to the ocean. As we walked in the pleasant cool of early morning, I knew there was something keeping us apart. I was not about to say what she was expecting of me. At least, not before the other question was settled. And I was thinking how much we are our own worst enemies, with our fears, our scruples, our conventions, not to mention our superstitions.

We reached a crossroads. I released the mare; at once she began cropping the fresh grass on the slope.

'I find it very hard, Isabelle, to put into words what I have to say to you.'

I felt I was talking like Rantanplan a little while ago. She placed a hand on my arm, her lips and her eyes smiling beneath the parasol.

'Really, Nicolas?'

I found myself thinking angrily that we were like two actors trying to exchange dialogue from two different plays.

'Listen, Isabelle . . .'

She dropped her arm and started toying with the folds of her skirt.

'Listen, Isabelle, let's get this question settled once and for all. I'd like us to be agreed upon something that's bothering me . . .'

She looked me straight in the eyes and I had to turn my face away to say: '. . . about the punishments to be inflicted upon the slaves.'

I sensed the absurd element in this conversation and it made me flush right up to my hair. Isabelle was staring at the tip of her shoe. She had taken a defensive pose, with her right foot slightly forward to keep her balance. The expression on her face had changed. It now had a closed, obstinate look.

'What do you mean exactly?' she said.

I plunged into an explanation: 'You know that for many years at Girofliers, corporal punishment has been abolished. I for my part am very happy about that. It would have been impossible for me to order the flogging of one of my men and to supervise it.'

'No one would have expected you to supervise it.' She had an ironic smile on her lips with their down-turned corners.

'I should like this custom, Isabelle, to be extended to the people on your estate.'

The riposte came like a whip-lash: 'They're *my* people.'

I felt a bit like a boy caught out doing something he shouldn't. 'You understand perfectly well what I mean.'

'I can assure you I do not, Nicolas.'

'Don't play wordgames, Isabelle. I'm sorry I did not make my feelings on this subject clear to you . . .' I was choosing my words and enunciating them awkwardly, in a hurry to get it all over as she gazed at me with her mocking smile. She moved away a little, then came back. 'Am I to understand that you are already cognizant of the order I gave concerning Introuvable and that you are criticizing me for it?'

'I think there's just some slight misunderstanding, Isabelle.'

'Do you know Introuvable abandoned his work and refused to start again?'

'Allow me to answer your question with another: do you know the reason why he abandoned his work?'

'His wife had had a baby. Every day babies are being born in the Grand Port camps. Do you think that's sufficient reason for the fathers to down tools and refuse to work?'

Her face had a hard look as she glared back at me; then she turned her back on me, tore the rib from a sugar-cane leaf and using it as a hunting-crop started lashing her skirt with it as she came back towards me. The sight of us standing there like that arguing at a crossroads seemed to me to take on the quality of a symbolic image. The mare continued to crop the grass peacefully. From time to time she stretched her neck between the sugar-cane stems, delicately selected some choice plant, then raised her head with a defiant air.

'What is your decision, Isabelle?'

'You are the master, Nicolas, and the one to decide what should or should not be done on your land. I wanted to preserve discipline which I considered useful. You are not of that opinion, so I bow to your decision.'

No matter if she felt her method had been preferable. It was an error she would get rid of in time. Doubtless Charles Ghast was not slow in lifting his hand to these slaves. But the image I kept in mind of a somewhat mean-spirited man appeared disagreeable to me at the very moment when I was about to indulge myself in the bliss of recollection. I placed my hands on Isabelle's shoulders and I felt the warmth of her flesh under the dress. We gazed into one another's eyes.

'Isabelle,' I said, 'not having you with me under the same roof when I wake up is something I can no longer accept.'

A sudden flush spread over her face and she half-lowered her eyelids. I left her and went to take Taglioni by the bridle. We came back by the same road towards the labourers, without speaking, as if everything had been said between us and accepted.

The slaves were continuing to sow the field. Two or three blows of the pick for a shallow furrow, three seeds of maize placed in a triangle, and the earth lightly covering the seeds. When we reached the field, I gestured to Tournesol to come forwards. He approached us, his eyes uneasy under the conical straw hat, his long frock-coat tails flapping against his calves. 'Tell Introuvable I've some urgent work for him to do. Ask him to go and wait for me at Girofliers.'

Isabelle, her shoulders rigid, lips compressed, took no notice of us. She turned her gaze back upon me when Tournesol had disappeared at the end of the footpath.

'This sort of dependence won't take us very far, Nicolas.'

'No, Isabelle, it won't take us very far, will it?'

I started to laugh, and seeing her frowning eyebrows and the rictus on her lips, I understood that one had to make great allowances for the problems of a woman who still could not distinguish dependence from love. But do not felines use their claws without wounding themselves?

By now the sun was fairly high in the sky and it was beginning to get hot.

'It's time to go home.'

She did not reply. She twirled the parasol on her shoulder and started walking quickly. At the first turning to Girofliers, I took my leave of her. She smiled goodbye and I got back in the saddle. I tried to distract my thoughts from a reality that was still unsettling me. I had put a rein on Isabelle's will, and for better or for worse I had forced my own will upon her. She could not forgive me for that, or at least not just yet.

I rode back to Girofliers whistling a tune. I had called for Introuvable and didn't know what kind of work to give him. I'd leave that to Rantanplan. Perhaps he could employ him in the garden. We were going to plant potatoes for the first time and had already begun to give the ground its second digging.

As soon as I got back, I began to sort letters received during the past weeks and to reply to them. By the last ship from France, I had received a long letter from Jean Desprairie, in whose charge I had left my affairs. He wrote about the practice, gave me the gossip from Saint Nazaire, mentioned the old woman who was caretaking the family house and ended by asking if I had finally chosen between the stuffy office and life in the open air. I wrote back that my choice had been made and that I was the most fortunate man on earth. I added that he could already consider himself the successor of the Kerubecs, notaries at Saint Nazaire.

Rantanplan served luncheon with a radiant face. I gathered that

Introuvable was in the basement. After dessert, I asked Rantanplan to bring him up to me. I saw a young slave of about twenty come in, with an open face and an intelligent expression in his eyes.

'You can set him to work on potato-planting in the garden,' I said, 'unless you have something else in mind.'

'Perhaps he could also run errands?'

'Very well,' I replied, 'he can start by carrying to Mahébourg the letter I've put on my desk.'

It was decided that in future Introuvable would live in the Girofliers camp. When Rantanplan came back into the dining-room to serve the coffee, I asked him for the keys to François' pieces of furniture upstairs.

After my siesta, I went up to the first floor. François' room was just as he had left it. The bed was made, the french windows were open on to the balcony, the furniture was gleaming. There could be no more poignant experience for me than having to look at that room and tell myself its master had gone out one day never to return and that it was I, a stranger after all, who was going to scatter to the four winds things that had been an intimate part of his existence. I leaned over the balcony before starting on my task. After living for one year in this house that had been his, amidst his staff, and after one year of intimacy with neighbours who had been his friends, I realized that I really knew nothing about my cousin. I had heard none of those anecdotes, none of those stories that reveal the man as he was, with his qualities and his defects, his courage and his weaknesses. Except for Madame Boucard *mère* and Rantanplan, no one had talked to me about him in any detail. Monsieur Boucard admired him and said so. It would seem as if he had not existed for the young girls or even for Isabelle, who had had fairly good relations with him from what I had understood, but who never mentioned his name. The forty-three years of his life had been spent within these walls. He had touched this furniture, had slept in this bed, had sat at this desk, had opened this wardrobe, chosen these clothes. And now it was all over.

I tried several keys before succeeding in opening the wardrobe. The clothes were carefully folded on the shelves. I placed them on the chairs. It seemed to me as if their fabric was still warm. A dumb grief weighed down upon me and once again I was disgusted by the injustice of fate. Who was I, what had I done to deserve to take his place like this, to be the beneficiary of long years of labour and thrift, when the natural heir, brutally severed from the joys he had created for his own pleasure, was now sleeping beyond the stream, with a hole through his chest?

In the drawers had been arranged his cravats, handkerchiefs and papers that to me had no value whatsoever. A receipted hotel bill, the programme for a day at the races in 1830, the draft of a contract for the purchase of a property of 120 acres, the name of the property left blank; brief notes authorizing patrols in such and such a district, convocations from the Civil Commissioner . . .

I called Rantanplan and asked him to make a bundle of François' clothes. He looked at me with loyalty in his eyes: 'It's a very painful thing for me, master.'

'For me too, Rantanplan,' I replied. 'But I could not put off this moment any longer. I shall ask Madame Boucard to distribute these clothes among the poor families of Mahébourg.'

He began packing everything into one of my bags that he went to fetch from the attic while I was opening the drawers of the desk. Some of them were empty, but one of them contained curiously worked pipes with blackened bowls. In another I found strange-shaped sea shells. Treatises on astronomy had been filed away in another drawer. The pages of these volumes were yellowed and it looked as if they had been consulted a lot. The colour plates held my attention for a long time. The majority of the plates had been indicated by bookmarks, used envelopes or simply bits of white paper. It was in the second volume I looked through that I found the letter or the draft of a letter: 'It's impossible for me to go on fighting like this with you and with myself. If I just stick to the facts, if I reject this fear, this doubt, this obsession, all becomes simple and easy . . .'

Rantanplan closed the bag and asked me if he should sent it to Madame Boucard. I replied that I must first warn the old lady and that I intended to go there myself that afternoon. I took up the letter again. I heard Rantanplan's footsteps dying away gradually.

> . . . I'll let the months drift by, I'll let time do its work and one day the moment will come. The moment will come when this need for you that took hold of me one night shall be fulfilled. Don't tell me you didn't know I was close by, in the shadows. I shall not believe you. You had slipped out into the avenue, you went down to the beach and you knew full well that I would follow you. A woman coming out of the water, who does not know she is being watched,

does not wring her hair so provocatively. You had just arrived in the flower of youth. Almost ten years ago. Ten years during which I have watched you living a life of your own. I told you; I told you that no other woman could ever exist for me. And yet, at that moment, you were still inaccessible. Yes, everything would be simple and easy today, if I did not tremble at your self-assurance, if I did not have to tell myself that I must never dare question you.

The letter was in my hands; I did not grasp its meaning entirely. To whom was François writing; to whom had he remained stubbornly faithful for ten years? I tried to remember the women I had met at the neighbours' houses, at Ferney, at Beau Vallon . . . I tried to visualize their faces, their figures, but even then I knew that this determined ransacking of my memory was only a pretence, a device, and that in all conscience I was just not letting myself give a name and a meaning to this sudden and brutal anguish that was overwhelming me. I went out on to the balcony. At the end of the avenue, the ocean was flashing under a pitiless sun and fringes of white foam crowned the breakers. The breeze from the open sea crested the smaller waves with spray. 'You had slipped out into the avenue, you were going down to the shore . . .' And without transition another phrase came back to my mind: 'There's a marvellous spot near here . . . In the past, from time to time, I used to enjoy bathing there after dinner.'

I sat down on the threshold of the french windows and drew long breaths of fresh air deep into my lungs. I got the impression that life had slowed down in me, that I had to struggle to shake off this chaos of confused thoughts whirling round my brain. I was still holding the two pages.

XXVI

I tied Taglioni to the hitching-post at the garden gate. Madame Boucard *mère* was sitting on the veranda. Was it intuition on her part, or simply coincidence? She announced at once that she was alone, that the other members of her family were spending the afternoon at Riche-en-Eau. 'As you are here to lend me a stout arm to lean on, we'll go down to the bench on the shore.'

We walked slowly as she recited the names of all the roses in the garden; I was only half listening to her. We passed a slave who took Taglioni's bridle and led her to the stables. As soon as we were seated facing the ocean, I told the old lady the purpose of my visit. 'I think it will be easy for you to find some worthy family to whom these garments will be of use.'

She laid a hand on my shoulder. 'You followed my advice and it cost you some suffering?'

I nodded; we sat motionless and mute gazing out to sea. I thought it would require only one or two questions . . . I folded my arms. 'Don't you find it strange that I should be replacing, at Girofliers, a man about whom I know nothing, except that he was my cousin, that he was young, unmarried, and that he died assassinated?'

She sat up straight and looked me in the eyes. 'Most people have no history, Nicolas. Look around you, there are so many who are born and die without anyone being able to find anything of interest in their lives.'

'But a being like François was different from others.'

'What makes you think and say that?'

I sketched a vague gesture. 'Perhaps a kind of intuition, or the idea I have of him as a strong personality, if I can judge by what I know, by the books he chose to read, by his studies . . . He studied astronomy, didn't he?'

'That is so, he had a passion for that branch of science. We often heard him talk about the planets, but what really interested him were the nebulae. He never tired of talking on that subject. I can never hear anyone name a star without thinking of François.'

She fell silent, cast me a look out of the corner of her eye and I knew that we were both thinking of our night spent aboard *Le Chevalier*. And no doubt we were both hearing the same voice reciting the names of all the stars. To my surprise, I found myself calculating the time I should need to assign its rightful value and its true meaning to that letter or that draft of a letter . . . I raised my head, and asked: 'Have you never heard people say, did you never guess that François was . . . in love?'

'Can one live to be forty, Nicolas, and never know love?'

It was no answer . . . that question answering my question was a gentle hint for me to mind my manners. For just one second, I was tempted to ask the old lady: 'Help me,' but I knew that no one could help me and I was not master of a dead man's secrets.

Two bulls, escaped from a nearby pasture, were wandering along the shore, advancing into the waves and drinking the salt water in long draughts.

'One thing is certain, Nicolas,' went on Madame Boucard. 'François was a man of intransigent honesty.'

Honest to the point of having lived ten years in the most total solitude so as not to offer any woman a heart overflowing with love for another. And for the first time, I allowed myself to accept the thought of that implacable question: 'And what did *she* think about it all?' I tried to play Don Quixote: 'She didn't even know!' But that sentence that left no doubt dogged my memory: 'I told you; I told you that no other woman could ever exist for me.'

And she had never, except on the evening when I was introduced to her at the Hôtel Masse, she had never pronounced the name François. Too preoccupied by everything she was bringing to my life, I had not stopped to think of that fact. It seemed natural to me that only those who had shared my cousin's life, who had tended his well-being – Rantanplan and a few others – that only they were authorized to speak to me about him with true familiarity, regret and pity.

A black ran past, stick in hand. The two bulls had wandered away slowly in the direction of Mahébourg.

'It's normal for you to feel sad, Nicolas, after dredging up so many memories,' said Madame Boucard. 'You had put off that decision quite long enough. But all is well now. Tomorrow you'll be yourself again.'

I gave a tolerant smile. I had to remain silent, explain nothing. Still try to put things in order within me, around me. Just as we were taking leave of one another, I thought of the long hours awaiting me before I would go to bed still without having had the courage to confront the problems. I could not admit to myself that those hours of solitude and the battles I must wage against anguish and memory frightened me less than the prospect of being with Isabelle, my heart filled with doubt and bitterness.

We watched the guardian of the bulls lift his stick, inviting his beasts to go back the way they had come. In the casuarina trees, the birds were beginning to gather for the night. The hint of a breeze released an odour of brine and tar. The tide was going out and the sound of the surf on the reefs had died away.

'I don't know what's tormenting you, Nicolas,' Madame Boucard said suddenly, 'but you must keep this always in mind: François can by no means be held responsible for anything whatsoever.'

What she was saying was not related, was not yet related to the thoughts that troubled my mind. I did not reply. A little later, when the bulls had gone past, guided by the slave, I asked Madame Boucard if I could leave Taglioni in her stables. 'I should like to go to Mahébourg on foot. I'll have someone bring her back tomorrow morning.'

I accompanied Madame Boucard as far as her garden gate. We had found again a certain liberty of spirit and speech. We talked of the sugar-cane cutting and the coming garrison ball, then I wished her good night. I turned away from the gate, but she called after me: 'Nicolas, come back here.'

I turned back. The old lady was picking from a bush a rosebud that had barely opened. She placed it in the buttonhole of my lapel and moved away, seeming to want to judge the effect produced by this touch of scarlet on the grey material of my jacket.

'There is in man fifty different possibilities of love – think about it, young man.'

And without further ado she turned on her heels.

XXVII

I walked to Mahébourg along the shoreline. I was quite aimless. I thought I might ask Monsieur Lepagnez to give me dinner, to linger on afterwards, and not return to Girofliers until midnight.

At the inn, I was greeted by welcoming cries; loud thwacks resounded on my shoulders. I was given a seat at one of the gaming tables and lost fifty piastres, word of honour, without batting an eyelid. Nor did I have to be asked twice to down heady draughts of brandy, but at ten o'clock I left the inn completely sober, dissastisfied, seized by a sudden longing for silence and solitude. Once more, I went down to the beach. The moon was half concealed behind a cloud. I sat down on one of the rocks left by the retreating tide. I was overcome by a great lassitude. I sat there a long time, elbows on knees, face in hands. Perhaps Isabelle had come out to look for me – perhaps, at this precise moment, she was wandering down the avenue, approaching my terrace . . . And I began to struggle with myself, struggle against this desire to thrust aside everything that kept returning to my memory, against the need for her that was dominating everything. Everything.

I let my hands drop. The sombre mass of the Mont du Lion stood out to my left. The boats anchored near the shore were softly rocking and the waves were slapping their sides. 'It's impossible for me to go on fighting like this with you and with myself. If I just stick to the facts, if I reject this fear, this doubt, this obsession, all becomes simple and easy . . .' Those words written by another's pen and addressed to a woman – I made them mine that night and I welcomed them, thinking of that same woman. Like François, I was fighting against my doubts and my fears: against an obsession. If I in my turn could just stick to the facts, everything would be simple and straightforward. But what was François fighting against? I felt sorry that I had not thought of bringing my pipe when I left Girofliers. I did not smoke it often, but I felt that on this night to stuff the bowl with tobacco, to light it, to draw on the smoke, would have been so appeasing, and perhaps comforting. 'Yes, today everything would be simple and straightforward, if I did not tremble at your self-assurance, if I did not have to tell myself that I must never dare question you.'

I understood that I should never escape all that. Never. That the letters would assemble themselves all on their own. That the words would form themselves implacably in my thoughts until I finally mastered them. I stood up and began to walk up and down the shore, my hands behind my back. Then the voice of Rantanplan re-echoed through my mind. 'He would sit at the desk for hours, arms folded, neither reading nor writing. Then he would start pacing up and down . . . in this room or on the terrace.' I went and leaned against the trunk of one of the mangrove trees bordering the shore. I could not allow myself to be like François, I could not allow myself to relive the hours he had lived through. I wanted to show I was more powerful, more strong-minded.

A horse neighed in the distance and suddenly it felt cooler. I turned up the collar of my riding coat and my fingers encountered the rose Madame Boucard had placed in my buttonhole. What a mockery! I tore out the flower and threw it on the sand and it seemed as though this angry gesture soothed me. With a heart still giving out great heavy beats, I took the road to Girofliers. I passed through the sleeping little town. From behind garden fences, dogs barked as I passed by. Through muslin curtains, I could see children's nightlights burning. In the Hollanders' street, a window opened and a man leaned out; he remained leaning on his elbows, watching me move away. Soon I had left behind me the little cobbled streets and I set off along the national highway. A gentle breeze rippled through the sugar-cane leaves and their frail shadows danced along the road. It was a night made for joy.

Before reaching the spot where Isabelle's avenue joined the main road, I slackened my steps. When I arrived in front of the gate, I stopped altogether. There was no light behind the windows: all I could see was, quite clearly, the house at the end of the courtyard, under the radiance of the moon. On each side of the drive, the poinsettias were waving their great arms, their flowers like hands, drenched in poison. I watched these branches rising and falling and I got the impression that I was plunging deep into an abyss in an endless fall. I had just begun to understand and accept the torment François had known.

XXVIII

Perhaps I ran to get back to Girofliers, perhaps I returned at a measured pace. Dawn surprised me still fully dressed. I could hear the familiar sounds of birds flying from branch to branch, Enclume shoving the dough into the oven, the slaves calling out to one another.

I took a cold shower, letting the water ripple across my face for a long time. I wanted to be like those insane people who howl without knowing why, but who nevertheless have the right to howl in order to rid themselves of their anguish. I regretted having left Taglioni at the Boucards'. No other saddle horse pleased me as she did, probably because I had purchased her myself; she was accustomed to my hand and my voice, and I only had to lay my forehead on her neck to feel her trembling with joy.

I was present at the call to work. After two days of sun, the drainage had started again on the ponds under the supervision of Vigilant. Nothing had changed. Rantanplan had served me breakfast before doing his rounds and I was left to choose between lounging about in the house or going in search of adventure.

I drank two cups of coffee without milk and Rantanplan looked at me in astonishment. I had the feeling I was spinning like a weathercock, deprived of either will or brain, no more than an animal living for the moment, with from time to time (to remind me of my existence as a man) the application of a branding iron on my bare flesh.

I went to fetch my old pipe from the bedside-table drawer and settled down on the terrace. I did not want to submit to the temptation to go for a long walk to calm my nerves so I perched on the balustrade, my legs dangling outside.

Then, like a child absorbed in a game of patience, I began to classify all the details that came crowding into my memory one by one. I made no allowances for myself or others. I assigned to each gesture a significance that I guessed at or invented, to each act its train of premeditation. I took pleasure in recreating the story of a woman who gets her claws into a vulgar brute for the simple reason that the creature possesses one hundred acres of land by the sea, thirty slaves, a house and cattle. I took pleasure in imagining the arrival of that woman on foreign soil, her reactions, her early curiosity, her first sight of a house that has something of the air of a manor. The sea-bathing by the light of the moon, the dripping hair . . .

'. . . A woman coming out of the water, who does not know she is being watched, does not wring her hair so provocatively.' And in the same hand, ten years earlier: 'Do you know anything more beautiful, more uplifting than drops of water running down bare skin?'

Then, the years going by, waiting with patience, perhaps resignation. Or the slow unfolding of an emotion or of some other ambition. The evening at Beau Vallon, the stroll in the garden between two dances. 'I told you; I told you that no other woman could ever exist for me. And yet, at that moment, you were still inaccessible.'

The return in the phaeton, at night, to a man she could not love, and the memory of another in his evening dress. The return, the door that opened on a drawing-room in whose four corners 'huge red and pink flowers, poinsettias, loomed up out of the vases'. Perhaps a cup of fatal herb tea which, the doctor said, 'gives no warning and spares no one'. At dawn, when it was all over, and the parquet cleaned: 'water was spilt all over the floor . . .' the slave sent for help to knock on the neighbours' doors. And the months passed by. 'Yes, everything would be so simple and easy today, if I did not tremble before your self-assurance, if I did not have to tell myself that I must never dare question you.'

I did not take it any further. No one would ever tell me: it's true; or it's false. And by a strange reversal of events I started thinking of my own arrival in the colony, of that concatenation of circumstances . . . A cold rage seized me and I kept repeating to myself that I had been duped, duped, duped – like François, like Charles Ghast. The presence of Isabelle in the Hôtel Masse on the day I disembarked now, to my newly awakened eyes no longer had the significance of a coincidental meeting. I was sure that the journey in the stagecoach was only the final stage of a cold calculation. I compared her devoted care for Madame Cochrane with the command to punish a slave with thirty lashes of the whip because he had too openly expressed his natural paternal feelings.

I decided to go and fetch Taglioni myself. On the road and along the shore I walked slowly. It was a morning like all other mornings, the sun continued on its course, the fishing boats were anchored by the reefs, the birds were singing in the trees. Entirely alone, I felt at a loss, aimless. Entirely alone, I was afraid of myself and of others, of what I was thinking and of what others might know.

At the Boucards' I called the gardener as I did not want to disturb anyone. However, as I was waiting beside the fence, I saw Anne coming towards me, her long pale tresses floating freely behind her. She seemed the very incarnation of youth and serenity.

'You pay court to grandmamma in our absence, Nicolas,' she said laughing, 'and you quite turn her head. All yesterday evening, she spoke only of you, at least so it seemed to us, for her sentences were disconnected and appeared to have no meaning except for herself.'

'Your grandmother is most kind to take such an interest in me, Anne,' I said. 'May I know why she shows so much concern about my well-being?'

'How should we know, Nicolas? She speaks about being blinded and thumps her fist on the table, then sticks out her chin saying: "Not afflicted with blindness all that much, after all." I was scolded because I burst out laughing.'

'I don't understand.'

'Nobody understands, Nicolas. And the more uneasy she feels you to be, the more she tries to unsettle you. But grandmamma's soliloquies and indignant outbursts have never harmed anyone. This morning, she's humming to herself all the time.'

I allowed myself to enjoy the company of this youth and freshness after the feverish night I had spent. The gardener, holding Taglioni by the bridle, came out of the stables and into the road. I looked at Anne and suddenly began to remember our last conversation. 'Anne,' I asked, 'will you answer me if I ask you a question?'

She seemed taken aback, then said calmly: 'And why shouldn't I, Nicolas?'

'Why did you talk to me about money and bank accounts last Saturday?'

'Why . . . for no reason, Nicolas, it was just a joke.'

She turned away her head, but I felt myself overcome by an urge to know.

'It was no joke,' I said, 'you had some reason. Was it not rather because you had had the opportunity, no matter how, to verify certain declarations you believed to be false, and which indeed were false?'

'I did not verify anything. I read a letter quite by chance, as it had no envelope. Just so as to find out to whom it was addressed, so that I could give it back. It was at Port Louis, when we were staying there.'

'Was it fifty thousand piastres?'

'It was fifty thousand piastres. And now don't ask me anything more.'

Her cheeks suddenly flushed and her eyes gleamed. Once again I felt an immense need for solitude. 'Au revoir, sister Anne,' I said.

She closed the gate behind me and leaned her face against the bars. When I was in the saddle, I turned back towards her. She raised her hand and waved goodbye to me.

I returned to Girofliers. When the stable lad came to take Taglioni, he ran his hand along the sweat-soaked neck of the mare and shook his head reproachfully. I did not usually demand so much of my horses and I understood his silent criticism.

In the library I waited in irritable patience until Cupidon had taken his broom and feather duster and left the room. I lay down on the couch, arms crossed behind my head. My cold anger of the morning was followed by a heavy sadness, then by a boundless forbearance. I countered everything I brought to mind with a firmly argued explanation and a plausible clarification. An hour passed by, then another. Ready now to make a decision in tranquillity and silence, I felt no longer quite as sure that a decision was necessary. 'I let the months pass by, I let time do its work . . .' A superior and magnificent blindness was leading me back into a world that twenty-four hours earlier had still been mine. An unspeakable happiness, a deceptive hope overwhelmed me, made my hands tremble. A brief fluctuation. Ballet de Rosine woke me from my reverie.

'It's Vigilant, master. He'd like to speak to you.'

I stood up and went out on to the back terrace. A relative quiet reigned over the outbuildings. The heavy work had stopped and the lunch hour was approaching. Coming out of the basement, Vigilant was coming up the back steps. 'We found this when we were dragging the pond this morning.' He unrolled a big leaf from a breadfruit tree and handed me a pistol covered with mud.

'Thank you for bringing it to me, Vigilant.'

He bowed, embarrassed. 'I thought maybe it was the pistol that . . . It's the pond right next to . . .'

I had then given Vigilant some tobacco and once he had left I started to clean the pistol as I waited for Ballet de Rosine to announce luncheon. I put the gun in a bowl of water and the coating of mud fell away. On the grip, two initials were clearly engraved. I went on cleaning it. I spun the cylinder. There was no bullet in the barrel.

I lunched with the pistol on the table, resting on a centrepiece of massive silver. When I had finished, taking my time over my lunch, I sat at the desk in the library and dashed off: 'I'll be waiting for you at five o'clock beside the ponds. Nicolas.' The sealing-wax singed my fingers. I called the stable lad and told him to deliver the note immediately.

Without knowing quite why, I went through all the rooms one by one on the ground floor, sitting a few moments in each one. In the drawing-room, I paused before the panels that had been sculpted by François, then inexplicably went and leaned against a french window giving on the terrace, my eyes fixed on the road and on the ocean. Later, I crossed through the outhouses, entered the clove plantation and reached the rustic bridge over the stream. Roseapple trees were spreading their branches, from which the honey-coloured fruit hung above giant ferns. Dragonflies were flying from bank to bank of the stream, drawn as eagerly as the bees to the scent of flowering cloves and ready to speed off in a different direction at the slightest change of wind. I leaned for a moment on the wooden guard-rail. The bark, long since dried out, crumbled under my hands, the stream shimmered and sang. But I knew that this was not the place to stop – I had no doubt she would keep the appointment – and I left the stream behind me. The path went up a sort of hillock, went down and then went up again to bring me finally to the five tombstones. I sat on the mirobolano roots growing out of the ground where the tutelary foliage shaded the grassy knoll.

François Kerubec, born in 1710. François Kerubec, born in 1744. François Kerubec, born in 1788.

I pressed the tips of my fingers on my eyelids; small luminous discs and great bright flashes jostled with other images. They kept coming without any effort of my will. I did not resist. What was the use, since I knew that life was carrying me away down current as surely as the dry leaves of the roseapple trees were being carried away by the stream and down to the ocean. I accepted the reality resurrected by memory, jerkily, without sequence.

Teatime found me at table in the dining-room, confronted by a plum pudding. Under the gaze of Ballet de Rosine, I started playing out the mealtime ritual, eating slowly, pouring a second cup of tea. This day had to be in every way similar to those that had preceded it since my arrival. I had taken my pipe and the account books when Rantanplan came to talk to me about the work schedules for the next day. 'Tomorrow morning . . .' I said, hesitant, a little foolishly.

We made our decisions as usual. Just before leaving, Rantanplan asked: 'Is it true, master, what they're saying in the fields – that Vigilant has found . . .'

I did not let him finish. I opened the top drawer of the desk. I had placed the pistol there after lunch, with the engraved grip against the wood. Rantanplan leaned over.

'That's what he brought me,' I said, closing the drawer. What they are saying isn't true. I've examined the pistol: the bullet has not been fired. You can tell them it wasn't this pistol.'

'Very well, master,' he said simply.

Left alone, I pretended to work for another few minutes, then I closed the account books. The hours dragged on. I thought I had better go and take a turn on the terrace and another in the garden where they were preparing the ground for the potato-planting. The nutmegs that had set in February were now as big as marbles and the tarmarinds had little green sprouts along their branches. With each breeze from the ocean, the Cythera tree scattered a golden shower of its leaves. I thought that if he could return, pass across this threshold once more, the King's Steward would have reason to be satisfied. But as soon as I recovered from my astonishment at having a mind free enough to dwell on these things from the past, a dumb anguish, a poignant regret made me stand stock still for a moment, my eyes raised to the first storey, and to the windows of Catherine Couessin.

At four o'clock I shut myself in the bathroom and thus gained a quarter of an hour. I knew that ten minutes would be enough for me to check the work at the ponds. After putting on fresh clothes,

I began to wander round the house, opening one book then another.

'I must return it to her . . .' I did not pursue the thought, put the books back on the shelves, debated with myself for a moment, then went up to the attics. The sun was still shining through the skylights in long golden shafts and the same mysterious atmosphere prevailed. I opened the marriage chest. A delicate perfume briefly rose from it and faded away. I took the grey dress with the little rosebuds and laid it on the cradle, my eyes attracted by the sight of other garments, a sort of uniform and also a blue fabric. A piece of paper was stitched to the uniform. I had difficulty in deciphering the writing's faded ink: 'Uniform of the national militia, presented at Port Louis, Ile de France, by Chevalier de Ternay'.

The jacket and knee breeches were of a thick white cloth. A little green turn-down collar contrasted with the red lapels and facings. François II's militia uniform. I unfolded the blue material and thought that this dress must also date from the period when the same François II decided to 'take him a wife' as was written in the family record. Out of curiosity, I spread out the dress on the parquet, to pass the time. Laid out like that, it strangely resembled . . . I turned round. I took the grey dress and placed it next to the blue one. Except for the colour and different decorations, they were in every respect identical – the same length, the same slender waist, the cuffs just as close-fitting. The long, wide skirts were mottled, and on the blue one there were little spots of mould, as if one night had not been enough to dry it after a thunderstorm's heavy rains. As if, still damp, it had been hastily stuffed into this chest one morning at dawn, before the first rosy flush began to rise above the ocean.

Before leaving the house, I slipped the pistol into the pocket of my riding coat. Once more I went over the rustic bridge, walked along the grassy knoll, cut across the fields. I had chosen this route deliberately, to take up time, but when I arrived at the ponds my watch still did not show five o'clock. I stopped at the very spot where François' body had been found. I leaned back against the trunk of a camphor tree. In the declining day, the humid breath of earth rose to my nostrils. Alert for the first sounds of feet moving stealthily over the grassy path, I watched the splashes of sunlight playing on the branches, caressing the buds, making the red camphor leaves flash vividly. But she was suddenly there without my having heard her coming, without the least snap of a dry twig under her light-soled shoes to give me warning. She was here, the rebellious little curls aureoling her face, eyes wide open, a trace of a smile lifting the corners of her mouth. I did not move, just watched her coming towards me, wondering if we'd have to waste a lot of time before we came to a definite understanding.

XXIX

'I was given your message, so here I am, Nicolas.'

Her smile widened, uncovering brilliant, uneven teeth, the two incisors in the middle well set, but the two others a little recessed.

'You're one of those women whose courage stops at nothing, Isabelle.'

At the first frown, the first inquiring look, then at the sharp pain that cut my breath, I became conscious that the hardest fight would be the one I had to wage with myself so as not to relent, not to give myself up to the delirium of temptation. I deliberately curbed my feelings, sought and rediscovered the atrocious image that had stamped itself upon my mind a few hours earlier and for a moment had to close my eyes.

'What's the matter, Nicolas?'

I noted the disquiet in the sharper tone of her voice and forced myself to assume a semblance of ease. 'Nothing.'

I put my hands in the pockets of my riding coat, touched the pistol.

'Nothing – or so little that, if you will, we shall not mention it. But I should very much like to ask you some questions.'

A wary look came over her face which had lost its smile and a little of its brilliance. 'What about?'

I ignored the question, holding out my open palm on which lay the pistol, its barrel blackened by the waters of the pond. 'For a start, I should like to know if you recognize this?'

She bent over it, seemed to have difficulty in recognizing it, then said very quickly: 'It's my pistol, Nicolas – you found it in one of the ponds, didn't you?'

'How did you know it was there?'

She had adopted a distant, impenetrable air, and I thought of the letter: '. . . if I did not have to tell myself I must never dare question you . . .' But I had promised myself that I would prove more powerful, more strong-minded than François.

The reply came in a natural voice: 'Because I threw it in myself. It's not a . . .'

She baulked at the word, did not utter it, but it was as present between us as if it had rung out under the camphor tree's foliage.

I regained the advantage and gave her a detached look.

'Perhaps it is . . .'

Her eyes gleamed with sudden fury, shifting nervously in the shade of her eyelids, and she moved towards me.

'You think . . . you think . . . Can it be possible that's what you think?'

I did not reply. I remained impassive too when she seized my arm and shook it roughly. 'And if I told you I got rid of it when they were making the house searches, would you believe me?'

A bird passed screaming over the trees, its cry reverberating. I had put the pistol back in my pocket and folded my arms. From the coarse bark of the camphor tree came a fresh, pleasant scent. Isabelle had picked up a small, dry branch and was tearing off its little twigs one by one. Lost in useless activity and contemplation that brought us to the point of mechanical courtesy, we nevertheless looked as though we were ignoring one another. A sudden gust of wind overturned all the leaves and made two closely growing branches squeak as they ground against one another. Isabelle shivered and raised her head.

'It's only the wind,' I said cuttingly.

She became aware of my presence once more, shrugged her shoulders and assumed an air of haughty contempt. She did not dare tell me she didn't understand, and countered my mistrustful hostility with silent indifference.

I had wagered on the surprise effect, but news spreads like wildfire from one camp to another, and Rantanplan, on his return, had not remained ignorant of Vigilant's discovery.

'For the past twenty-four hours I've been asking myself a question that is still unanswered,' I said.

She did not seem to hear my words. She was slapping her palm with the dry branch. I felt rising within me the need to strike her and wound her as I had been struck and wounded. I stood erect, feet apart, feeling the play of muscles under my skin.

'I'm wondering what your heart held more dear – the man (no matter which one of us), or what the man represented?'

This time, her lips blenched and she moved closer until she was almost touching me. 'I forbid you, Nicolas, you hear, I forbid you to talk like that. Is there nothing you respect?'

'Not when I think too much,' I replied. 'Since yesterday, I've had too much leisure, too many occasions to remember and compare.'

She controlled herself, releasing her breath slowly. A touch of red appeared on her cheeks and her eyelids fluttered. She turned away and went and leaned against the nearest tree trunk. If I had put out a hand, I could have touched her or even drawn her towards me.

'Perhaps I should have talked to you about it earlier,' she said. 'I think it's not too late.'

She was silent a moment, her sombre eyes fixed upon mine. 'Perhaps I should have told you that in the past there was . . . between your cousin and me, something that resembled an understanding.'

She fell silent, waiting for a movement or a word that did not come, so she went on: 'We did not talk about it, because it was only a few months after my husband's death. When François died in his turn, when I got back from Port Louis and they told me the tragic news, it seemed to me to be pointless to inform strangers of the projects we had conceived together. You knew, didn't you, that I wasn't here when it happened?'

'I knew that the next morning you departed by coach at dawn.'

Her eyes avoided mine, moved away from the path, gazed at something in the distance. She was probably looking at nothing.

'Whether you believe it or not, it was not until my return that I learned . . .'

I broke in: 'You needn't bother. What's the use? What I believe or don't believe is no longer of any importance . . .'

I felt an immense weariness, a need to be quiet, to stop thinking for a few hours, a need to plunge myself into my helpless despair. The main thing, I was thinking, is to get it over with. Whatever comes of it is not important. I just want her to understand that it's impossible to go on and that a decision . . .

I still did not realize that long before I had done so, she had understood and accepted everything, and probably better than I had. 'Everything. I don't want to keep anything. If one day, I were to decide to leave, I'd want it to be within the hour.'

'Nicolas . . .'

She had spoken my name in that marvellously deep voice that I had heard one night, one single night. Something too sweet and too insistent ran through me and for a moment left me laden with an incomparable happiness.

'Nicolas . . .'

I passed my hand over my face. 'That's enough of that!' I answered rudely.

But this time she was immune to attack, and the suspense enlivened her parted lips, the eyes looking sideways through her lashes.

I turned away. The memory of a night and two devastating days made the blood rush to my head. A fruit or a branch dropped somewhere into the grass with a dull thud and a chicken squawked. 'I just want her to understand that it's impossible to go on . . .'

'Didn't you lose something else?'

She had leaned back against the ebony tree, her shoulders back, head high. She was putting up a lonely and magnificent defence against the attack I was making on her.

'A blue dress? A dress which strangely resembles another dress with little rosebuds . . . that you left somewhere one stormy evening . . .'

She remained motionless, her hands clenched behind her back.

One by one the tears started running down her face. She went away as she had come, silently. A frail little figure that a curve in the path hid for ever.

The next day, at dawn, the trotting of four horses rang out on the highway and something like an echo or a sob trembled through the house.

The demesne sweeps down to the ocean. From the terrace I look at the long avenue of palms and mirobolanos that leads to the shore. Beams up in the attics crack under the sun. There are dresses, too, in a chest up there.